Steven Isn't Normal

Marco A. Vásquez

Floricanto Press

Copyright © 2014 by **Marco A. Vásquez**

Copyright © 2014 of this edition by Floricanto and Berkeley Presses.

All rights reserved. No part of this publication may be stored in a retrieval system, transmitted or reproduced in any way, including but not limited to photocopy, photograph, magnetic, laser or other type of record, without prior agreement and written permission of the publisher. Floricanto is a trademark of Floricanto Press. Berkeley Press is an imprint of Inter American Development, Inc.

Floricanto Press
7177 Walnut Canyon Rd.
Moorpark, California 93021
(415) 793-2662
(800) 523-3175
www.FloricantoPress.com
ISBN:13: 978-1-888205-51-0

"*Por nuestra cultura hablarán nuestros libros. Our books shall speak for our culture.*"

Roberto Cabello-Argandoña, Editor

Steven Isn't Normal

To Matthew and Mason, who will always hold my heart in their tiny hands.

Chapter I

Steven Meresko isn't normal. He's retarded. At least that's what people say. They say he is retarded because that's what he is: retarded. By definition, mostly, but retarded nonetheless. They say this as nonchalantly as they say that fat Consuelo is fat, crazy Pedro is crazy, or that old man Felipe is an old man. That is what they are. That is what Steven is. He's a retard. Steven doesn't think he's retarded. But that doesn't matter because nobody cares what Steven thinks.

Since his pathetic childhood, nobody has cared what Steven thought. All most people have ever known was that he was retarded, or so they say. People don't just say he's retarded. They also say that he's crazy, stupid, slow, idiotic, moronic, psychotic, *loco, menso, pendejo*. People have been saying these things about Steven, and directly to his face, for most of his life. By people, I mean his parents, siblings, friends, neighbors, teachers, business owners, passers-by—just about everybody that Steven has known, met, seen, or has heard of him. Steven doesn't know that so many people are calling him names. He only knows of a few. If he did know, he probably wouldn't care. He's used to it. He's heard it enough so that it no longer registers as an insult.

As a child, Steven was teased at school for his poor mental capacity and his extreme weight. His mental capacity was not based on academic potential. It was based on events. His extreme weight was due to the fact that he ate tremendous portions. His mother served them that way. Steven just ate them. His mother insisted that he eat everything on his plate before he would be allowed to leave the table. So, Steven would eat everything on his plate. He would do this with the fervor of somebody who was about to receive great compensation for a job well done. Unfortunately, that never occurred. He was just given temporary freedom.

In kindergarten Steven pissed himself in front of the class. It wasn't entirely his fault. His mother always gave him orange juice in the morning, along with three scrambled eggs, toast, and a pile of bacon. She insisted that he drink the entire glass regardless of his lack of thirst. He drank it. She also insisted that he eat all the food on his plate. He did, with his usual fervor.

That day, during recess, Steven was riding a silver tricycle around a white track that was crudely painted onto the rough, asphalt playground. His fellow students laughed at Steven as he rounded the corners—one wheel lifted off of the ground threatening to spill Steven's five-year-old, bulbous frame onto the floor. He never fell, but the anticipation was enough to even get his teacher to giggle and stop him.

"Careful, Steven. You don't want to fall and hurt yourself." She told Steven this every time he rode the tricycles. Steven knew he didn't want to fall. He knew he didn't want to hurt himself. Still, he stopped for the sake of eliminating any further criticism.

After riding the tricycle, Steven drank water out of the fountain that all of the other kids refused to use. A kid had stuck a twig into the fountain causing the water to come out at an awkward trajectory. Steven didn't care about the water's trajectory. He was thirsty. He drank the water. Because of the fact that none of the other kids used that fountain, Steven was allowed more time to drink water. He wasn't being shoved from behind. He wasn't being told to hurry. He was being pointed to and laughed at by the other kids for using the fountain that had a twig in it. It didn't bother Steven. Steven just drank and drank.

After recess, Steven's teacher gave him a carton of milk. Steven wasn't thirsty, but his teacher insisted that he drink it. So, he drank it in just a few large gulps that forced some of the milk to roll out of the corners of his mouth, cascading down his chin and throat, creating two dark pools on the neck of his faded, Navy blue T-shirt.

Within minutes, Steven had to urinate. He had to ask for permission to use the facilities. Steven's teacher had always told him to raise his hand if he had a question. Steven raised his hand. He kept it in the air, straight as an exclamation point, for what seemed hours. It only seemed like hours because the desire to urinate was so strong that it even changed his ability to sit properly. Hence, he was very uncomfortable for those few minutes that seemed like hours. He kept his hand in the air as he watched his teacher help another student replace eight fat crayons into a yellow and green box. He kept it in the air as he watched his teacher hold a child's finger and maneuver it over a piece of paper with a big black "R" on it. He kept his hand in the air as he felt his lap warm with liquid that was gushing out of his body, on his chunky legs, through his pants, onto his socks, the arches of his feet, and into the inner soles of his tight, tan Buster Brown shoes. He kept his hand in the air as the boy sitting next to him noticed the darkening of Steven's pants and the puddle that was forming at Steven's feet. He kept his hand in the air as the student sitting next to Steven announced to the class that Steven had pissed in his pants, to a sudden burst of laugher. He kept his hand in the air until the teacher finally turned to look at him, laughter in her eyes, and told Steven to put his hand down, which Steven did. She didn't ask Steven to state his question. She asked him to go and see the nurse. He did this with laughter behind him, steady as applause, as he exited the classroom.

From that point on, his fellow classmates started telling Steven that he had to wear a diaper, that he didn't know how to hold it in, that he smelled like pee. Steven didn't like the teasing much, but he didn't like it much when he was sent to the nurse that day and she told him the very same thing. He also didn't like it when he was sent home and his mother told him the very same thing. Nor would he have liked it had he known that, right after school, his kindergarten teacher burst into the teachers' workroom, laughing hysterically, barely able to tell all of her colleagues the story of the stupid kid that pissed himself. By the time his fellow students started teasing him, the words ceased to have much affect. He sort of ignored his fellow students. His ignoring them was translated into stupidity, or retardation, if you will.

"Don't you know that you're not supposed to pee on yourself? Are you retarded?"

"Yes." Steven was answering the first question. The students, naturally, assumed that the answer was directed toward the latter.

In the second grade, Steven had volunteered to participate in the spelling race. He was to race one of his fellow students, a girl named Barbara. Barbara knew she would easily win. She thought, "I'm going to beat this retard, easily." She did, although not as easily as imagined. The idea was that the teacher was going to announce a word. The first of the two students to spell the word correctly on the chalkboard would win. It was a very productive time in Steven's education. The teacher announced the word: chicken. Steven began writing, his left, meaty hand moving the chalk along the coarse, green board as quickly as he could. The fact that Steven was left-handed seemed strange to some of Steven's classmates. They would say things like, "You write weird." Steven didn't think it was weird. It was just natural—as natural as anything Steven or anybody did or learned. As Steven was writing the word on the board, some students were looking at his left hand. Steven was, also. He was writing fast. To everybody's surprise, especially Barbara's, Steven and Barbara finished writing at the same time.

"Okay. Let's see," the teacher said. She had to check for spelling. That was a rule, after all.

Barbara spelled the word correctly. Steven, on the other hand, spelled "*chichen*." He had forgotten to put the little line above the "h" that would have made it a "k." Naturally, the classroom laughed at Steven as loudly and steadily as they did that day in kindergarten. The teacher even laughed as she shook her head and asked Steven to sit down. Steven sat down. To make matters worse, fried chicken was being served in the cafeteria for lunch that day, so all of the students couldn't help but say things like, "Are you going to eat your *chichen*?" "This *chichen* tastes nasty," "I don't like *chichen*." They made sure to say these things loud enough so that Steven, and as many other people as possible, heard them and laughed. Then they would shake their heads contemplatively and say to themselves, "Sheesh. *Chichen*? What a retard."

"Steven is retarded." They would say this to his face, to their friends, to their teachers, to their parents. Eventually, it caught on, and stayed with him throughout his years at school.

In fact, now, in his late twenties, Steven is known as "Steven the retard" around his neighborhood. Only now, Steven is retarded. Steven still doesn't care what people say. The neighbors call him a retard when he's walking down the street: "There goes Steven the retard." The neighborhood children call him a retard when they see him on his front yard: "Hello, Steven the retard." The mailman and ice cream man deliver the same salutation: "Hi, Steven the retard." That's what Steven hears. They don't always say "Steven the retard." Not to his face, anyway; not all the time. They sometimes just say, "There goes Steven," "Hello, Steven," "Hi, Steven." Steven always hears the addition of "the retard" because he's heard it all of his life.

Steven tells his mother that everybody calls him "Steven the retard." Steven's mother, Martha, acts surprised when she hears this, even though she already knows that they call him a retard because Steven has been telling her so for over a dozen years. She's overheard the neighbors talking of Steven in that fashion. In fact, she has called him a retard countless times, along with stupid, idiot, moron, *tonto, menso, pendejo*.

She called him stupid the first and only time that Steven told her what he wanted to do when he grew-up. Steven was twelve when he told her, "I want to make Coca-Cola. I want to work where they put the Coca-Cola into the bottles." He said this after watching the opening credits for a Laverne and Shirley television show rerun.

"That's stupid." That was all she said. Steven never said anything else about it.

Steven's mother, as a superficial means of consolation, tells him not to listen to what people say about him, that one day, he'll be normal again. She says, "Don't listen to what people say. One day, with the help of Jesus Christ, my Lord and Savior, you'll be normal again." Steven's mother is a devout Christian. She was reborn a Christian after her Catholic first husband, Rogelio, died. Until then, she was a devout Catholic. Back then, she believed that Christ, with the help of his virgin mother and a handful of saints, would help make Steven normal. Now, she believes that only Christ will make Steven normal. Steven believes that he already is relatively normal— that is, as normal as anybody else. He doesn't tell his mother this. He just listens to his mother's constant reassurance. He knows his mother's words are free of tenderness. He knows his mother's words are merely a front, a distraction, a way of getting Steven to drop his guard and to trust her. That is why he decided to kill her.

Chapter II

Steven Meresko was born Esteban Meresko. He was also born perfectly healthy, along with a twin brother named Boris. Steven was given the name Esteban because both of his parents have Mexican roots. Boris was given a Russian name because their father, Rogelio, had a Russian ancestor on his mother's father's side. Steven's father refused to let that fraction of Russian DNA go. There was Russian in him, after all, no matter how minuscule the proportion. Even his last name was Russian, to some extent. Still, it sounded Latin enough so as to not stir any question in the small Mexican town where Steven's father was raised. Steven never had a problem with his name or family name. He had problems with his disposition. That always seemed to be a problem. The problems eventually escalated. In fact, it wasn't until Steven had the horse-riding accident that things really changed.

The accident happened in Mexico, in the small town where his father, Rogelio, grew-up: Jocotepec. Steven's neighbors from down the street, the Chafas family, also have roots in the same town. Neither family knows of this. However, Steven's father and the Chafas' patriarch would occasionally eyeball each other, and each would say to themselves, "I think I know this guy from somewhere." While neither ever asked the other, both were somewhat correct. While they never knew each other personally, they happened upon one another as often as one would living in a small town in Mexico.

Nonetheless, that was where the accident happened.

As a child, Steven's father, Rogelio, was very fond of horses. Rogelio's family only had one horse, so his great fondness was directed at that one horse that they named *Tope*, as in speed-bump, on account of a bump he had near his hind leg that, while it didn't limit the horses speed and mobility, was an undiagnosed, malignant tumor. With seven brothers and one sister in the family, Steven's father made sure that it was he who brushed, fed, and gave the horse plenty of water from the farm's well, giving Rogelio a greater sense of ownership. He would ride the horse on his family's farm. He liked riding the horse, fast, down a narrow dirt road, lined with trees, digging his booted heels against the hard waves of the horse's ribs until Rogelio's eyes squinted due to the wind, and all his ears could hear was a whistle. Rogelio never forgot that youthful sensation. He always wanted his son to experience this with him.

Steven's family had taken their usual biannual vacation to his father's hometown of Jocotepec. It was a biannual trip because Steven's father, Rogelio, was the sole provider for his family. Steven's mother, Martha, wasn't employed. Her job was to cook and clean, and to raise the children. While some women may say that running the household as a homemaker was a job in and of itself, Steven's father, Rogelio, would never say this. It was her lot in life, and that was that. It was the role granted to her upon marriage. It wasn't exactly a politically correct way of looking at one's wife, but it was the way that they had determined upon marriage. And, by "they" I mean "he."

Rogelio's job was to discipline his children, and he

did. Rogelio was also a plumber. While plumbing can be a lucrative career, it wasn't for Rogelio. He wasn't licensed, and didn't speak a word of English. One would think that Rogelio would seek Spanish speaking clientele. He did. Only the Spanish speaking clientele refused to pay Rogelio the exorbitant prices that he set, which were suggested to him by his bilingual contemporaries. The clientele insisted that he lower his prices because they would never pay so much for a service that could be performed by a bottle of Liquid Drano. Rogelio never budged. The idea was that eventually somebody would bite, and that would hold the family over until the next month. Eventually enough money would be saved for airfare, and not much else, which was why they always went back to the farm where they could sleep for free and eat for very little else.

Steven was thirteen years old when they took their fateful trip to Jocotepec. He wanted to ride a horse, but having been born and raised in East Los Angeles, he never had the experience. The only horses Steven had ever seen were on television, painted onto the sides of pick-up trucks, and the white ones in Tijuana, Mexico, that were striped with black spray-paint in order to look like zebras, and stood on the corners, much like their prostituting counterparts, waiting for tourists to drop a few American dollars for a photograph. Steven's brother, Boris, was not interested in the horses. Boris preferred the company of his mother.

Rogelio decided that he and his son, Steven, would ride on the same horse this time, despite Steven's increasing weight problem. Martha never allowed her husband to take Steven on the horse before because Steven was too small—

she was afraid he would get hurt. Rogelio figured that his son was ripe enough, and he certainly wasn't getting any smaller. They had to ride as a pair because there was only one horse to ride. It wasn't the same horse, *Tope*, that Rogelio rode as a child. That horse was long dead. As luck would have it, that horse was struck by the truck of a neighboring farmer that was hauling two ponies that two of his own horses birthed just two weeks prior. The farmer couldn't believe his misfortune. The farmer was speeding on his way to another farm to sell the ponies when he struck Rogelio's horse as he, a teenager, was walking the now-limping beast along the side of the road. Rogelio thought he was lucky that he wasn't riding the horse. Rogelio felt luckier when the farmer offered to replace the dead horse with one of the ponies. The dead horse was taken by the farmer and sold to the local butcher for meat. He wasn't about to leave the dead horse sprawled on the road like a speed-bump, or a *tope*, if you will. The farmer later went home, driving much more carefully, with only a little bit less money than he would have had he not struck *Tope*.

  The horse they would ride together, *Relámpago*, which means lightning, was the very pony that Rogelio was given by the farmer that struck and killed *Tope*. It was old, but it was still strong enough to hold Rogelio and his son Steven, regardless of Steven's weight. Rogelio would sit on the saddle and control the horse because he was an experienced jockey. Steven had to sit on the horse's rump, just off of the saddle. Steven was told to hold on tightly, and to not let go, no matter what, as they trotted toward the familiar narrow, dirt road that Rogelio always grew nostalgic for when away from his hometown. Steven held on tightly.

Rogelio dug his heels into the horse's ribs, the way he did as a child, and the horse ran. Rogelio felt the wind in his face. His eyes squinted like never before, tears blurring his view. The whistle in his ears was louder than ever. It was so loud that he wasn't able to hear his son screaming.

Steven, while holding on tightly to his father, was slowly sliding off of the horse's rump, his body jiggling and bouncing, out of rhythm with the horses ebb and flow. Only, he wasn't sliding back, toward the horse's tail. He was sliding sideways so that his right leg was curling underneath, along the horse's belly. Neither the galloping horse, nor Steven's nostalgic father were aware of this. Steven was aware. That was why he was screaming. His body had slid so far that his fatty frame was at a right angle to the horse's body. He kept yelling with fear that, at any moment, his face would meet the narrow, dirt road, and his body would roll with the force and momentum of the horse's speed. He was also yelling because they were coming upon a eucalyptus tree with limbs that extended onto their path. Rogelio saw the tree's foliage-heavy limbs and thought it would feel great to brush against the cool, green leaves, that his son would get a kick out of adding another element to an already perfect experience.

Steven screamed. He screamed until the split second before his forehead hit a tree branch. Then he screamed some more as his mind went blank before he relived the experience in his head as a series of close-ups and color-flashes.

Rogelio stopped soon after he no longer felt Steven's sweaty grip on his shirt. He looked back and saw his son on the ground. Steven's father turned *Relámpago* around with such a yank that the horse did most of the turn in mid air. He raced to Steven, his senses not as considerate of the wind. Rogelio knelt beside Steven. Steven had a bump on his forehead, blood threatening to burst out at any second. It didn't.

Steven opened his eyes and saw his father.

"Are you okay, son?"

"Yes." He was okay, as far as he knew, though his head was throbbing so much that he could feel the huge bump continuing to grow on his forehead, and he could swear he felt his skin stretching there.

It wasn't until Rogelio insisted that they climb onto the horse and return to the farm that things went from bad to worse. Rogelio got back onto the horse. Rogelio extended his left arm to allow Steven a bit of leverage. As Steven attempted to climb aboard on the left side of the horse, Steven's weight, and Steven's father's weaker left arm would not allow Steven to be lifted. Naturally, Steven decided to try getting up on the horse's right side. The horse was not aware of the various factors that were going on around it. All *Relámpago* felt was a body walking near its tail. The horse instinctively kicked a hoof that brushed against Steven's flabby chest, caught some loose skin and his left arm, and sent him flying. The hoof hit Steven's arm as solid, Steven imagined, as if he had been struck by lightning. Steven fell hard onto the ground. The side of Steven's head hit a sharp rock that had been half-buried in that very spot, exposed a little every year when the rains came, for years. That rock changed Steven forever.

As it turns out, the sharp rock hit Steven at such a precise location that it would impair his speech for the rest of his life. The town's doctor was very concerned about the bump on Steven's forehead. The doctor didn't give the cut on the side of Steven's head much attention other than a cleaning and a bandage, unaware that that blow had left damage as permanent as the sharp rock from which it was conceived.

It wasn't until days after the accident that Steven's speech changed. His voice sounded the same, but he had slowly developed a stutter so severe that it made most of what he said incomprehensible. Occasionally, he could spit out a comprehensible word, but, for the most part, Steven's speech was words that were turned to garble once they left his mouth. Such was the beginning of Steven's actual retardation. The one good thing that came of this incident and newly developed retardation was that Steven would no longer get teased at school. His mother insisted that he no longer attend school for fear of ridicule. That is, more ridicule than before the accident.

Aside from his speech impediment, Steven is also schizophrenic. He was diagnosed at nineteen, six years after his accident. Steven's mother, Martha, swears that the horse riding accident had everything to do with Steven's schizophrenia.

"He's mumbling all the time, doctor. I don't know what he's saying. It was that bump on his forehead. I know it was. Damn his father; God rest his soul. Jesus Christ, my Savior, help me." The doctor smelled beer on Martha's breath. He raised an eyebrow, but didn't mention it. She looked at Steven who was sitting on the examination table, then back at the doctor. "He cries and cries for what seems like days in a row. I'm not sure, because I'm at church, but when I leave he's crying and when I get back home, he's crying. I don't know why he cries. God help me." She looked back at Steven. She was starting to cry. "Why do you cry, Steven?"

"With a . . . With a . . . Me, my, my, my, me. With a . . ." Steven was trying to say that sometimes he cried because he didn't know what else to do, and that other times he cried because he just felt like crying.

"You see what I mean, doctor? I can't get a sentence out of him. I don't understand. Jesus, Lord, my Savior. He cries. He locks himself in his room and doesn't come out for days. Other times he leaves the house and doesn't come home until late at night. Some days, he yells at me and his stepfather. Other times he's just fine. But still, I don't know what he wants or needs. It was the horse accident. It was the bump on his forehead. He's never been the same. I just pray to Jesus Christ, my Savior, everyday that he helps me."

The doctor that eventually diagnosed Steven after a series of evaluations and referrals told Steven's mother that schizophrenia was genetic, but Martha wouldn't listen. She kept damning Steven's father for making her suffer the humiliation of raising such a child. She prayed to Jesus Christ, her Savior, for the strength to nurture her retarded son.

"Jesus Christ, my Savior, I ask you for the strength to raise my retarded son," she said the minute she and Steven got into the car and drove home from the doctor's office.

Steven's mother considered institutionalizing Steven. She didn't know what else to do, or any other way of freeing herself from this burden. She considered a place that a church going friend of hers once mentioned. It was a place called the Anne Sippi Clinic, located in the rolling and gang-banging hills of El Sereno, California, which is in North-East Los Angeles. The Anne Sippi Clinic was not known for the woman after whom it was named. In fact, if you asked any of the employees of the clinic who Anne Sippi was, they'd just say, "Look, I just work here." That much was true. What was also true was that the Anne Sippi Clinic was known for its late-night screams of terror, and the fact that it helped schizophrenic patients. Steven's mother didn't know any of this. She only considered sending Steven there briefly. That is, the consideration was brief, not Steven's potential residency. She knew that, with enough faith, there were other ways to help Steven.

According to Steven's mother, with the help of Jesus Christ, her Savior, and the government of the United States of America, she should have the strength to raise Steven. She does have said strength. All she has to do is see to it that he takes his medication every morning, and that he eats. The doctor made it presumably clear that it was important that she give Steven his little, blue pill at night, so that he can sleep well. The little, blue pill that he prescribed was Stelazine, but Steven's mother got its generic form, Trifluoperazine, because it was cheaper. It was cheaper in price, not effectiveness, she figured. Nothing is too good for her son. She didn't listen to the doctor's orders. She gives him one little, blue pill every morning, the only one he needs. She assumed a morning dose is the same as a night dose. After all, the pill doesn't know what time it is. Fallacies aside, according to Steven's mother, the logic is sound. So she does that much. And, she feeds him. It doesn't take much strength, but Steven's mother still huffs and sighs whenever she has to give Steven his little, blue pill and his food. The government takes care of Steven's inability to be a productive member of society by providing him, by way of his caregiver, a check for seven hundred dollars a month. All Steven's mother had to do was keep him alive. One could say that Steven's mother has been doing a stellar job of keeping him alive. At least, it would appear that way. After all, he is alive.

She keeps Steven alive by feeding him burritos. She makes them out of chorizo, potato, and eggs. Steven doesn't really like chorizo, but he eats the burritos, anyway. He doesn't have a choice. Steven's mother would make a large pan of chorizo every Sunday, allowing the fatty, spicy pork to breakdown in the pan before adding the potato and eggs to the rendered bits of meat and drippings. She would feed herself and her husband, and stuff the rest into a dozen tortillas. She leaves an uncovered plateful of chorizo burritos in the refrigerator and tells Steven that he has to eat one every morning and one every evening. Steven does. He eats one every morning and one every evening. Occasionally, he would tell his mother that he didn't like chorizo, but his mother wouldn't understand him.

"No . . . No, no, no. No. I . . . No." Those were the words that came out of Steven's mouth. Steven's mother could not make any sense of them, so she translated Steven's words into what she thought he was saying.

"It's not too spicy. Just eat it. Praise the Lord for the food that you eat." Steven did, eat the burritos, that is. He even ate the burritos that, as the week went on, started to absorb the smells of everything else in the refrigerator; the burritos that tasted less like chorizo, and more like the smell of a late afternoon burp of someone who had chorizo for lunch.

Along with the burritos and his little, blue pill, Martha gives Steven forty cents each day so that Steven can buy himself a candy. When she doesn't have change, Steven gets a dollar. Martha doesn't know that forty cents a day will not get Steven a candy at any nearby store, much less anything else. That was why he locked himself in his room for days. He really had no choice. He had to save for several days in order to have enough money to do anything. In fact, Steven has been saving his money for months. He has a sandwich bag under his mattress filled with coins and bills. He has plans for that money. Martha used the remainder, after giving Steven his allowance, of the seven hundred dollars that she gets for Steven from the government each month on donations to her church, where she would pray for Steven, when she wasn't praying at home. Her constant praying has made Steven suspicious. She doesn't tell Steven that she is praying for his well-being and normalcy, and for the good Lord to free her of the weight and humiliation that her retarded son is causing her. All Steven hears are whispers through the living room window addressed toward a porcelain statuette of Jesus Christ, bearded, in a white robe, arms open. Steven doesn't know exactly what she is saying to the statuette. He hears his mother whispering, but whispering with such zealousness that it must be more than just the usual banter. He hears the statue whispering back, and his mother responding with more zeal and his own name being exchanged. He thinks that his mother and the statuette are plotting something against him. He isn't exactly sure what they are plotting. He has his ideas, though. If his ideas are correct, then he has no choice but to kill his mother.

Chapter III

Steven lives in his mother's garage. The garage is not attached to the house. The garage has been converted to suit people rather than cars. The walls have been covered with drywall to hide the wooden frame and the garage's one window. It would have been too time-consuming to cut the drywall and fit it around the window. So, now, from the outside, through the window, all one could see was the other side of the drywall. Besides, windowsills would have to be considered, and that would have meant careful, time-consuming planning. The floor has been covered with linoleum, bubbling at spots where the adhesive didn't quite catch because of the oil-stains on the concrete that once supported a truck. There is a small bathroom sectioned off that has a stand-up shower and a toilet. Steven has a twin bed, a chest of drawers, and a twelve-inch, black and white television. This is Steven's sanctuary. Martha insists that he not enter her house for any reason, except to get his food. The reason being is that since Martha re-married, after the death of Steven's father, Rogelio, she has become highly sexual. That is to say, she wants her privacy.

Steven's mother, Martha, married a man named Bob that she met at a local bar called Tony's Hof Brau. She met him there one Friday night when she happened by for a drink after her usual Friday evening prayer group. The rest of her prayer group went home to continue their prayers. Steven's mother, the drunk that she is, wanted a change of pace. Usually, following the prayer group, she would stop at Art's Liquor for a twelve pack of Budweiser. She would then take the twelve-pack home and drink as much as she needed to fall asleep. Sometimes it took six cans of beer. Other times it took nine cans of beer. Very rarely did it take the entire twelve-pack. When it did, Martha woke-up the next morning and prayed to Jesus Christ, her Savior, that he give her the strength to restrain herself because nine beers should really be enough.

Bob was sitting at the bar sharing a pitcher of Budweiser with nobody, just like he hadn't shared the two pitchers that he had already finished. He was wearing black cowboy boots, jeans, a white T-shirt, tightly pulled over his belly, with a puffy brown vest over it. Steven's mother sat next to him and ordered herself a beer.

"Tony," she told the bartender named Art, "Can I get a Budweiser?"

Art, the bartender, didn't correct her assumption. "Bottle or pint?"

"Glass, please."

As Steven's mother finished her pint of beer, Bob, with what little mental capacity that was left in his drunken, balding head, partially refilled her glass with what was left of his pitcher.

Bob told Steven's mother, Martha, that his life-long dream was to become a police officer, that he was single because his wife left him five years ago for another man. Martha told Bob that she was a widow of ten years, and that she hasn't met a man worth talking to until that night.

That was all it took. They did their little ritualistic dance—more talking, a pardon for an accidental bumping of knees, a hand on the lap. By the end of the night, the two of them had gone through several pitchers, then went home and screwed.

All the while, Steven was in his garage, listening to his mother screaming in her room, "Oh, God! Oh, God! Jesus! Oh, God!" Steven didn't know what to make of such adamant prayer, but he was waiting for his own name to be screamed. It wasn't.

Ever since, Martha has held on to Bob. Actually, it was more like Bob held on to Martha. Although, he would never let Martha know this. He insisted on maintaining his archaic masculinity by convincing Martha that she needed him more. He would do this by pointing out how attractive other women where, especially those on television. That was enough to make Martha feel just inadequate enough to allow herself to believe that she needed Bob in her life more that he needed her. She did want him in her life, after all. That's why Bob didn't work. He didn't have to. That, and the fact that he continued to maintain the ridiculous idea that he wanted to be a police officer. But, at fifty-nine years old, his chances of actually becoming one were non-existent. His age wasn't the only factor. Bob was fat to the point where it turned his walk into a robotic wobble. Bob was also a drunk. Bob stayed home all day watching small claims court television shows and episodes of Cops that he recorded every Saturday night, drinking beer after beer. "Research," he called it.

Martha didn't work. She had a savings account filled with the insurance money she collected after the death of Steven's father. She would go to the bank once a week, and withdraw several hundred dollars. That was all she and Bob needed. She never asked Bob to get a job. His conversion of the garage where Steven was sent to live was work enough. She never even considered getting a job herself. She had all the money she needed. With Bob in the picture, she even had the luxury of sex. With him home all day, everyday, she had the added luxury of sex anytime she wanted it. For that, she thanked God. "Thank you, Jesus Christ, my Savior, for bringing a loving companion into my life." Indeed.

  Because of the fact that she can have sex at any given moment, she insists that she and Bob remain naked throughout the day. Then again, Martha has always had a fascination with nudity. Only her fascination had never involved herself. When Steven and his twin brother, Boris, were very young, she insisted that they walk around naked. Not just around the house, either. She insisted that they walk around the front yard and sidewalk naked, never straying too far from their home. She enjoyed seeing the two boys skipping, hopping, and running around the lawn, genitals bouncing to the rhythm of their movements. It was nothing perverse. She just enjoyed seeing her children in the most natural of ways. Steven and Boris didn't mind it too much. They were only four or five years old. They were young and it felt rather refreshing, especially on those warm Southern California summer afternoons. What Steven did mind was when the neighborhood kids would put twigs and cigarette butts between his ass cheeks. Boris didn't mind it so much, but Steven did. He also didn't like the fact that people would laugh whenever they saw him and Boris running around naked. Steven and Boris didn't know any better. Martha knew better, but she kept them naked anyway. She would make sure that they were completely dressed by the time their father got home. She knew her husband wouldn't be too fond of that. And the kids never said anything to their father. Not knowing any better, what was there to say?

While the practice of having her nude children running around the neighborhood eventually stopped, Steven's mother's fascination didn't stop. That is why Steven is not allowed into the house, except to get his breakfast and his dinner. Other than that, Steven can only be in his garage. He has, on dozens of occasions, spotted both his mother and Bob, through a window, frolicking around the house naked, sitting on the couch naked, grabbing beer from the refrigerator naked, refrying beans naked, opening mail naked. Bob caught Steven's stare once and matched it with such a severe stare of his own that Steven had to look away. Although the sight of a naked Bob should have been enough to make Steven avert his vision, the unusual sight made him maintain his view a split second longer just to make sure he wasn't seeing things. Steven finds this lack of undergarments bizarre, and hopes to, one day, correct it, in order to help his mother.

Bob doesn't really mind being naked all day. If his wife insists that he remain naked, then he shall remain naked. The only thing Bob insists is that his wife not hang any pictures of her deceased husband in the house. It isn't that Bob is insecure. He's going to be a police officer some day, after all. It's just that it sort of creeps Bob out. Her husband is dead. He should no longer be a part of their lives. That's Bob's logic. Because Martha respects her loving new husband's wishes, she took down every picture of her dead husband. She didn't have much of a problem with it. In fact, she took down just about every picture of her family. The only pictures that remain on the wall are pictures of her and Bob's wedding and a solitary picture of Steven.

What Bob doesn't know is that Steven's mother has a large stash of photographs of her dead husband in her underwear drawer—she has plenty of room in there. It's her secret stash that Bob doesn't know about, and she hopes he never finds out. She fears that he might some day find out because of the inquisitive nature that she believes he has, due to the fact that he wants to become a police officer. What Steven's mother doesn't know is that Bob isn't aware that Steven's mother even owns a pair of underwear, much less has an entire drawer devoted to them. As far as Bob is concerned, if the pictures aren't hanging, they don't exist. The only pictures that Bob thinks exist are the picture of his wife's retarded son and the pictures of their wedding day.

The picture of Steven was taken long before his accident. The picture that hung on the wall was one of Steven when he was one year old. He was smiling like a normal child, propped-up against a vanilla background, with a vinyl Mickey Mouse doll on his lap—the paint on the dolls ears chipped away by Steven's young teeth, his little outfit one size too small forcing his baby arms to pillow at the biceps. Other than that, not another picture of Steven was anywhere in the house. In fact, Steven's mother never considered photographing Steven after his accident. She didn't want to see any pictures of her son after he ceased being normal.

The rest of the pictures were of her wedding with Bob. It's obvious that all of the pictures on the wall were taken on the same day. The reason it is obvious is because in every picture, Bob has a huge, bloody bandage around his head. You see, Bob was in an accident on the day of his wedding.

The morning of the wedding, Bob had several beers after taking a shower, before putting on his suit. The beer sat so well that Bob fell asleep on the couch. When he woke up, he realized he was running late. He threw on his shirt, grabbed his tie and coat, and jumped in his car. He was rushing to the wedding's location, the American Legion Hall in Montebello, California, imagining that he was in hot pursuit of a criminal suspect. While the name of the hall suggests a hint of sophistication and prestige, it is just a fancy name for a big, empty room with wood paneling on the walls. That day, the room was filled with friends and family, all eagerly awaiting Bob's arrival. They waited longer than they thought they ever would, the guests whispering to each other, looking at their watches, and shrugging their shoulders. As it turns out, Bob was in such a rush that he failed to time his left turn, which caused another car to slam into his car's passenger side. Bob slammed his head against, and through, his driver-side window. Hence, the bandages. While the paramedics that assisted him on sight insisted that a doctor check him out, Bob assured them that he was all right. They believed him, and left the scene, as did Bob, his car still able to putt along, albeit with a bit of a vehicular limp. All that remained at the scene of the accident were bits of glass that littered the intersection. By the time he got to the American Legion Hall, his wife-to-be was crying, thinking that she had been jilted. Bob had blood all over his left shoulder of his white shirt, but his coat covered that up. All he had to do was wash the dry blood that had dripped down the side of his face and neck. The blood that was seeping through the gauze around his head would eventually clot. The ceremony and reception went on. The photographer immortalized Bob and Martha: husband and wife. That night, during the reception, Bob continually joked about his wrapped head by saying, "I'm practicing for my job at Seven-Eleven." Everybody, including Bob, laughed. Everybody laughed because Bob looked like an Arab, and continued the joke with a few more racial slants that involved camels, crashing airplanes into buildings, and sand. Bob laughed because the thought of ever getting a job was silly. The only work he ever really did was the conversion of the garage into Steven's room. And, as simple as that was, it was enough for Bob to consider himself retired.

As decent as the conversion of the garage into Steven's room went, the room has since become filthy. Steven doesn't clean it. Steven's mother doesn't clean it. The room has remained untouched by a mop or dust-rag for the ten years that Steven has occupied it. There is a thick layer of dust on top of his wooden chest of drawers, making it appear as though it is a counter in a kitchen that has been prepared for the rolling of pizza dough. There are several stripes of dust that have been swept away from certain spots where his fingers accidentally touched it. In the top drawer, Steven has accumulated just about every little, blue pill that his mother has ever given him. Steven's mother doesn't know about this. She figures that they go straight into his mouth and get distributed by way of his bloodstream toward their designed destination. They don't. Steven doesn't like to take the pills because they make him sleepy, which is why the prescription called for a nighttime dose. Once Steven gets handed one of the little, blue pills, it goes straight into his left pocket, then into his top drawer.

There are probably hundreds of little, blue orbs scattered throughout the drawer. Luckily they are small. Otherwise the drawer would be overflowing with little, blue pellets. Along with the pills, Steven has a stash of dozens of pairs of women's underwear: briefs, thongs, lacey ones, silky ones, pink ones, purple ones, yellow ones with the crotch permanently stained and stiffened by dried blood that came sooner than anticipated. Steven doesn't wear them. He steals them from the neighborhood women that hang them on clotheslines and leave them on the cinder-block walls and chain-link fences to dry after being washed, scrubbed at crucial spots. Steven is collecting them to give to his mother who, according to what Steven has seen, is in dire need of them.

Another thing Steven collects is his own boogers. He doesn't have a regimented way of keeping and cataloging them. He simply sits in his bed, picking his nose, and wipes them on the wall just above his head. There must be thousands: some small, some big, some long, some dry, some flaky, some bloody. Steven doesn't care much about his collection, but he is always careful not to accidentally peel any off when he wipes on another.

Steven's floor is covered with footprints and traces of spills that have spread into the chaotic shape that gravity gave them, that have since dried into sticky, black ghosts. There are cobwebs that nearly create arches at every perpendicular corner of the ceiling and an army of dust-bunnies lined against the walls pushed there by an occasional gust of wind created by an opened door. The stench from the bathroom permeates the entire room. It smells as though the toilet has never been flushed, along with the lingering moisture of a moldy shower that festers due to the lack of ventilation caused by the lack of any windows. The trashcan by his toilet is overflowing with wadded toilet paper. The paper at the very bottom of the can has been sitting in there for years and has since taken the shape of the trashcan's base. The funny thing was that Steven didn't even need to have a trashcan next to the toilet. It would have been perfectly fine to flush all of that paper away with all the shit that was flushed down. The trashcan is only advisable if the premises use a septic tank to house the waste. Steven's house did not have a septic tank. Steven's mother just put the trashcan there out of habit, or for mere aesthetics, if a trashcan made for toilet paper can be aesthetic. The bathroom floor is a mess. Along with the toilet paper, there is enough pubic hair on the floor to fill the head of a bald, black man. The toilet seat and basin are stained with shit and urine. The bottom of the toilet seat is splattered with traces of the stool that occasionally is abnormally loose. The hole in the toilet that sucks Steven's waste is caked with green and black film, remnants of the countless chorizo burritos that Steven has eaten. Steven once walked into the bathroom late at night. When he turned on the light, he nearly jumped out of his skin when he saw the toilet. He imagined that the basin was the open mouth of a giant man threatening to crawl through his bathroom floor. He imagined that the hinges of the seat were the man's eyes, and the drain that washes away all of Steven's crap was the man's throat. He soon realized that it wasn't a man, but only his filthy toilet. That sight alone would have been scary enough for any person but Steven. Steven still had to look around the bathroom, before pissing, to settle his nerves thanks to the toilet-faced man he imagined. His shower door is surrounded with black mold that also climbs up the fiberglass walls, and the shower head is fuzzy with calcium, lime, and rust. Steven doesn't mind the filth. He isn't even aware of it, at least not the idea that somebody may find this lack of cleanliness abnormal.

The only clean thing in Steven's room is an old, plastic Mickey Mouse doll that Steven has had since he was an infant—the one from the picture. His father gave it to Steven after buying it at the swap meet. The paint on the ears of the Mickey Mouse doll has been chipped off ever since Steven went through his teething stage. Steven had forgotten the doll until it resurfaced in the garage. Bob was going to throw it out, along with a lot of other things that may have had familial value if Steven's mother had valued her family: baby shoes, certificates of live birth, dried pieces of umbilical cords in Ziploc bags. Steven found the Mickey doll among the garbage cans as he was sifting through them looking for glass bottles. Now, the Mickey Mouse doll is Steven's only companion. Steven sleeps with it and keeps it on his bed when he isn't in it. He pulls the blankets just over Mickey's red shorts, leaving Mickey's arms and gloved hands resting above the blankets. Steven talks to his Mickey everyday. It talks to Steven. Steven loves his Mickey Mouse.

Another thing Steven loves is glass bottles. His love stems from his idea of someday working for the Coca-Cola Company.

He has been collecting bottles for years. He keeps his stash at a secret, secluded location. He has clear ones, amber ones, green ones, long-necks, short-necks, forty-ouncers, thirty-two-ouncers, twenty-two-ouncers, twelve-ouncers. He has hundreds. He has them lined-up and separated by color and size two blocks away at the train tracks, against the back wall of the paper factory. Steven loves them as much as he loves his Mickey Mouse doll. He especially loves them when the sun strikes them at a particular time of the day: the light dimmed by the hues, and bending with the perfect curves of the translucent glass. He loves the colors and the reflection that his bottles produce at that particular time.

It was the Mickey Mouse doll that told Steven what his mother was up to. It told him, not in the squeaky, mouse voice that one usually associates with the mouse, but rather in a British accent. In fact, the voice he heard was the voice of the evil Emperor Palpatine, from the Star Wars movies. Steven didn't recognize the voice as that of the Emperor's. As far as Steven was concerned, it was Mickey's voice. It said, "Your mother is planning to take away your bottles. She wants to take them from you and give them to Bob as a gift." Mickey continued to tell Steven that his mother and Jesus were in cahoots, that Steven had to do something, that he had to stop her, that he had to act soon, that she was going to ruin his collection. All of this seemed to make sense to Steven, and he even wondered why he hadn't realized this himself.

One morning, Mickey told Steven that if he valued his collection, that he had no choice but to kill his mother. Steven only had to consider this briefly because he knew what had to be done. That morning was when Steven decided that he would have to kill her.

Chapter IV

Steven took a shower after he received direction from Mickey Mouse. He shaves once a week because after a few days his face grows cactus-like stubble that itches like mad. That day, Steven shaved because, although he had something to do for a change, his beard was itchy and prickly. He shaves with an old, rusty razor and lathers his face with a bar of soap. Steven doesn't like to shave because the dull razor snags on his week-long beard, pulling to the extent that it feels as though he is yanking out each follicle. Steven doesn't know that the razor is dull, nor is he aware that his beard wouldn't snag so much if he were to shave more frequently. But, he doesn't shave frequently because he's afraid of the pain that he feels when his beard snags. So, by prolonging the pain, he is increasing it. What do you expect? He's a retard. Along with the snags, Steven always ends-up with nicks at the base of his neck. He feels the nicks burn when he steps into the shower and the hot water strikes them with a steady, although inconsistent, stream.

Although Steven showers everyday, he still stinks. He stinks because he dries himself with a bath towel that hasn't been washed in ten years. The towel that was once soft, white cotton is now dark yellow and is turning gray along the edges, and has the rough texture of AstroTurf. Steven uses it because he is oblivious to the towels stench. He smells it, but figures the smell is coming from the disgusting toilet and moldy shower. While there is a foul smell always coming from the toilet and shower, and it is very similar to the stench of the towel, it is the towel that carries the smell that lingers along with Steven.

To make matters worse, Steven wears the same clothes everyday—the same pants, anyway. He has been wearing the same pair of jeans for the last five years. He had another pair of jeans that tore into long fibrous threads at the crotch five years ago. Steven's mother noticed Steven's need for new pants after Steven had been exposing his underwear through his crotch for several months. She wouldn't dream of having that. She didn't want any son of hers exposing his underwear. All or nothing.

Steven has several T-shirts that he wears for weeks at a time. They are all white, cotton T-shirts. They were white, at least. Now they are all nearly transparent as a woman's stockings, yellow and stiff at the pits, and slightly gray, like a cloud that couldn't possibly carry rain, but can precede one that may. He wears them everyday. His mother washes them once in a while, and even replaces them with new ones once in a great while. Steven doesn't consider their age or cleanliness. He wears whatever shirt he finds first. Usually it is the one that he wore the day before. This is apparent because there are usually browning bloodstains that have soaked into the neck, caused by Steven's shaving with his poor grooming instrument.

Like any person, Steven hasn't always had the capacity to bathe himself. Steven's mother bathed him up until only a couple of years ago. Bob didn't like the thought of his wife bathing her grown son. But, Steven's mother had to do it. She convinced Bob that it was necessary. Bob didn't need too much convincing. Bob figured the guy was a retard so he needed help of this kind, the way a quadriplegic would need similar help. His logic has never been very linear. Anyway, she started to bathe him after she noticed that Steven refused to bathe himself. She would force him into the shower in his underwear. She would rub his head with a bar of soap while Steven sputtered something about the soap getting into his eyes. He tried to sputter that. His mother just translated it as just another whine like that of a toddler that doesn't want to take a bath. The reason the soap got into Steven's eyes was because he didn't like to close his eyes in the shower. He always thought that if he closed his eyes for too long, he would open them and find somebody standing next to him. That thought always scared Steven. He never told his mother. She would probably say it was stupid.

She would.

He would put-up with the pain in his eyes. She would then rub the bar of soap against Steven's body until there was enough lather to spread with her hands. Then she would put the bar of soap inside of his underwear and maneuver it from outside his briefs, squeezing his cock and balls, sliding the bar of soap along Steven's ass-crack. She would then leave him alone to rinse and dry, Steven's tears invisible through the water pouring over his head. Steven's mother started bathing him shortly after Steven's Father, Rogelio, died.

Steven was fifteen the summer when his father, Rogelio, died. That is to say, Steven was fifteen the summer when his father killed himself. Steven doesn't know that his father killed himself. Steven's mother tells him that his father drowned in a bizarre accident that involved a dog bowl. The dog bowl belonged to Steven's dog, a Chihuahua he named *Chiquito*, which—appropriately enough—means "little." Steven believes the dog bowl story because he was the one that found his father dead. Steven found his father dead in the backyard, face down in *Chiquito*'s water bowl, though he didn't know the specifics. As Steven's mother tells it, Steven's father was mowing the lawn in the back yard on a very typically warm summer day. The heat was so intense that Steven's father fainted. As luck would have it, Steven's father fell, face first, into *Chiquito*'s water bowl. There, Steven's father continued to breathe, as any normal person who had fainted would continue to breathe, only his lungs and alveoli filled and were saturated with water, rather than oxygen. She added that had the dog's bowl been empty, or had Steven never gotten a dog, his father would still be here. But, it wasn't and he did. So, his father went to heaven, or so Steven's mother said. "His soul is in the hands of Jesus Christ, my Savior," she always told Steven.

Whenever she told Steven this story, Steven asked, "Wh-what . . .? Wh, wh, wh, what . . .? Wh-why?" He was trying to ask why his father didn't emerge from his fainting spell upon contact with *Chiquito*'s water. Steven's mother, obviously, could not make sense of Steven's gurgling. She told him, "He's with Christ, now, my Savior."

The day Steven's mother first told him about how the drowning may have been avoided, Steven marched into the back yard, grabbed *Chiquito*'s Chihuahua frame, and threw it against the brick wall. *Chiquito* never knew it was coming. In fact, as Steven approached the little dog, *Chiquito* was wagging his tail and licking its jowls with the thought that he was about to be played with or given a treat. Instead, *Chiquito*'s skull shattered inside of the skin that made-up its little head on contact with the wall, then fell to the ground silently as blood trickled out of its mouth and ears, its head still recognizable although deflated like a forgotten balloon. Steven felt justice had prevailed. Steven cried for weeks after that incident—not only for his father, but for his dog, as well.

Steven's mother never had the nerve to tell Steven the truth about his father. She couldn't, after what Steven had done to *Chiquito*. She couldn't tell him that Steven's father had been riddled with guilt for the past two years. She couldn't tell Steven that his father never got over the fact that he had damaged his child, the only one out of the four he had conceived that showed promise. He couldn't deal with it. So, like many people that cannot deal with the cards that life has dealt them, Steven's father took his life by drinking an entire twenty-ounce bottle of Liquid Drano. The Liquid Drano followed a liter of tequila that had been consumed just prior. The Liquid Drano didn't go down as easily as the tequila did. Still, Steven's father managed to choke it down, spitting some out of the sides of his mouth as he tilted the bottle back. It burned his throat a bit as it went down. But, Steven's father was determined. Together, the tequila and Liquid Drano created such a lethal mixture that Steven's father had taken in his last breath a split-second before his face hit the water bowl. In fact, his last breath exited his body while his face was submerged, along with a portion of his stomach's contents, which would account for the small pool of greenish-blue vomit that surrounded *Chiquito*'s bowl, and his father's head, like a halo. Steven was oblivious.

Steven did find it curious that his father died—as far as Steven knew—in a similar way that his grandfather, Rogelio's father, died. Steven's grandfather, Esteban, also drowned. Only Steven's grandfather didn't accidentally drown, nor did he kill himself. Steven's grandfather was killed. Rogelio told him the story once. As it turns out, Steven's grandfather was, much like his son Rogelio would turn out to be, a drunk. Often, he would come home to the farm late at night, drunk on tequila, vomit into the well, and beat his wife, Steven's grandmother, Guadalupe, before forcing himself upon her. Esteban never planned it that way. He was a thin, short man. He would get drunk at a bar where other men would push him around when they saw him advancing on one of the whores that frequented the bar. Esteban didn't want any trouble. He just wanted to get laid. The other men that were in the bar never let Esteban get any action. They always pushed him away from the girls, and laughed as his drunken, spindly body stumbled backward between wooden chairs and crashed to the damp, cool, concrete floor. Esteban couldn't retaliate because he knew that the bigger men would pound him. They would. He couldn't compete. So, he would continue drinking, avoiding any eye contact with the men and women at the bar. All the while, he would plot scenarios in his head where he actually beat the men over their backs with the wooden chairs and then swept the women over his shoulders, took them out back, and had his way with them. He would envision these events until he ran out of money. He would then go back to his farm, vomit in the well, then find his wife asleep and do what he did. Guadalupe's sister, Carmen, while not aware of the treatment he received at the bar, was well aware of Esteban's behavior toward her sister because she had been hearing about it for years. Carmen would tell Guadalupe that she shouldn't take that kind of abuse, that she deserved better, and that she needed to do something about it or he may one day kill her. This advice was quickly dismissed with a shrug and the words, "Oh, well. What can I do?" And, in small town Mexico, back in those days, that should have been enough to end that conversation. In fact, several times, that was enough to end their conversation. But, at one point, Carmen decided that if she and her sister were going to have any more conversations at all, Carmen had to do something.

  One night, the night of the new moon, while Guadalupe was sleeping, impregnated with a child that would be Rogelio, Esteban came home, drunk as usual, burping and preparing to vomit into his usual place. Only this time, as he vomited into the well, Carmen emerged from the darkness and pushed him from behind. Esteban fell crashing through the water in the well, head first, and nearly broke his neck. He would have survived had he not been so drunk. But, due to his inebriation, and the darkness of the night, Esteban, thinking that he was swimming up to the surface of the water, instead attempted to swim deeper. He didn't realize this until his hands were scraping dirt and gravel. At that point, he gave up. After a minute, Carmen heard what was sure to be Esteban's limp body break the surface of the water.

  Steven's grandmother got over the death of her abusive husband quite easily and eventually found herself in the arms of a married man. She would see him around town, buying candies and other treats for his children which accompanied him. She fell in love with him for the great father that he was to his own children. Steven's grandmother assumed that he would be just as good a father to her children. He was a great father, but the man's wife didn't care much for her husband's adultery. She considered killing her cheating husband when she found out about his adultery, but didn't. Instead, she produced more children with him because he was such a good father. It was her way of keeping him around. It worked. It worked so well that, after a few years, he stopped visiting with Steven's grandmother. She remained alone, a widow. Steven's grandmother, Guadalupe, eventually dropped her dead husband's last name and went back to her maiden name: Meresko.

Strangely enough, Esteban's brother, Steven's granduncle Nicholas, died in a fashion similar to Steven's father's actual death. While Nicholas killed himself, unlike Steven's father, Nicholas didn't kill himself on purpose. Nicholas was drunk. He was enjoying a drunken evening at the plaza of his native town: Jocotepec. He was sitting on a bench taking huge swigs of tequila straight from the bottle. There was a townwide party going on celebrating the Catholic Church around which the town was founded. He had to get drunk. A young shoe polisher named Pedro Chafas approached Nicholas and asked him if he wanted his shoes polished. Nicholas did. So Pedro Chafas went to work. Pedro Chafas was a proud shoe polisher. He had concocted a polish so potent and effective, it would easily remove the mud and cow shit that was caked on the local men's boots. The polish was black so it not only made the boots shine, it also filled in cracks in the leather making them invisible, and saturated any stubborn chunks of red earth and green shit so that they became invisible. Pedro Chafas kept his shoe polish mixture in an old tequila bottle that he had found in the trash. Coincidently, Nicholas placed his tequila bottle on the floor next to the bottle of shoe polish. As is quite apparent, Nicholas then accidentally picked-up and took a huge swig from the bottle of shoe polish. After several more swigs, Nicholas was on the floor in a pool of black vomit.

Steven didn't know about his grand-uncle Nicholas' death. He didn't know about his grandfather's murder. He didn't know the truth about his father. He didn't know about all of this death that seemed to plague his family's history. Nor did he know that if alcoholism and genetics have any validity he should be preparing himself for an inevitably long battle with cirrhosis of the liver. All he knew was that he needed to get his sandwich bag of money from under his smelly mattress, to set his plan into motion, and be on his way.

Chapter V

Steven got his sandwich bag of money from underneath his smelly mattress, stuffed it into his left pocket, and went outside. The day was sunny and very warm. Steven liked warm and sunny days because he knew that later, when he went to see his bottles behind the paper factory, the sun would shine through them and he would see the brilliant colors and the reflected light that he enjoyed so much.

As usual, when Steven went outside, he walked on the front lawn for several minutes, limping, rather, as Steven tends to do. He liked limping in circles, as he had seen his now deceased dog *Chiquito* do before it took a shit. Steven didn't shit after limping in circles. After limping in circles, Steven went and knelt near a rock on the grass under which, for the last couple of weeks, Steven had seen ants. The ants fascinated Steven, although he was deathly afraid of insects.

Steven's fear of insects comes from a dream that he had about a fly. In his dream, the fly was buzzing around his head, zipping and swirling, with an incessant agenda. Steven attempted to swat it away. After several misses, the fly managed to fly directly into its apparent target: Steven's ear. Steven tried to retrieve the fly from inside his ear, but as he dug his finger deeper into his ear, the fly was being pushed in as well. The fact the he always bit his finger nails didn't help his leverage. Had he even a sliver of nail, he would have been able to scrape the fly out, he rationalized in his dream. The buzzing became louder as the fly was pushed deeper. When the buzzing got to a level of sound that Steven could no longer stand, and when the panic of the irreversible depth that this fly had reached began to paralyze him, Steven woke with a scream, sitting-up in bed, breathing heavily, sweating. Steven dug his pinky into his ear. There wasn't a fly in there. He did, however, pull out a large wax nugget that he wiped against the wall with his booger collection, which was probably, along with a few overly-sensitive hairs, what had caused the discomfort that he felt was a fly. Needless to say, although Steven continued biting his nails, he always left his pinky nail on his left hand a little longer, should his dream manifest.

Another time, Steven had a dream that the hem of his blanket was covered with crickets. In his dream, he heard the crickets chirping, and saw them moving their legs in unison like a massive violin section. Eventually, the chirping got so loud that, with a scream, Steven woke-up, sitting-up in bed, breathing heavily, sweating. While there was nothing, in reality, going on in his bed that would justify such an illusion, he'll shake his blanket out with a rolling whip before lying in bed, ever since.

The thing is that Steven suffers from exploding head syndrome. Exploding head syndrome is the sensation one gets as they're falling asleep, where they may be dreaming that they're falling or in the midst of something uncomfortable and the brain, the bizarre organ that it is, suddenly wakes the person. It's a real thing. This always scares the shit out of Steven. So much so that Steven once shit himself after the syndrome awakened him. He dreamt that there was a cockroach crawling on his pillow, creeping toward his head. He heard the roach's legs tapping the pillowcase, and heard its little insect feet sinking into the pillow as it stepped closer to Steven's head. In his dream, he saw a close-up of the cockroach's legs pressing slowly into the pillow's fabric, as though it were tiptoeing toward his head, calculating each step so as not to accidentally wake Steven before the roach reached him. Again, with a scream, Steven woke-up, sitting-up in bed, breathing heavily, sweating. Only this time, there was a handful of shit in his underwear, so Steven ran to the bathroom. Remarkably enough, had he turned to look at his pillow, he would have seen that there was, in fact, a cockroach walking on his pillow. But, the darkness of the room, and the soggy lump in his underwear deflected his attention.

    He never had a dream that involved ants. He liked how organized they seemed to be. He remembers seeing a long line of ants carrying pieces of leaves and what looked like seeds. Curious, Steven followed the line of ants to a hole in the ground. Steven wanted to know what was in the hole, so Steven dug around the hole with a twig that he found nearby. Steven soon unearthed what looked like little white maggots, perfectly stacked and organized like hundreds of tiny bottles. Steven thought these maggots were some sort of ant food, but soon realized that the ants were kissing these maggots, or so it appeared to Steven. Steven found this beautiful. Steven soon pieced together the fact that the maggots were the larvae, or babies, as Steven thought, and the ants were not kissing, but feeding them. Steven was fascinated by the care and love the larvae were given even in the face of giant danger, that such a deep, bonding love could be shared between what most conclude were mere grotesque pests. While what Steven assumed was relatively correct—the ants were feeding their larvae—there was no care or love involved, and the ants didn't see Steven as a giant danger. Ant larvae secrete a sweet fluid that attracts the adult ants to them. They then release a larger portion of fluid from their mouths in order to get the adult ants to feed them. Clever. And the ants were right to disregard the potential of Steven's danger. Curiosity, not danger. Not to the ants, anyway.

Steven didn't know any of this technical ant business. He just liked watching the ants. He even told the ants, "I'ma . . . I'ma . . . Kill'em. Buh-buh-buy it. Buh-buy it." What Steven was trying to tell the ants was that he had to kill his mother, that he had some money, and that he was going to buy something that he needed in order to kill his mother.

The ants, like any human, could not make any sense of the noise coming out of Steven's mouth. But Steven thought otherwise. He saw how the ants, as they passed by one another seemed to glance over at each other for a moment and tell each other something. Steven figured that the ants were spreading the word about Steven's impending deed. Steven wanted this to happen. He wanted everybody to know.

After looking at the ants and telling them his plan, Steven went to the kitchen door and knocked on it. He remembered that he had his bag of money in his pocket, so he ran—as best he could—back into his room in the garage and threw the bag on the bed so that his mother wouldn't get suspicious of anything.

"Wha-wha. Wha . . . Watch," he told Mickey. He was telling Mickey to keep an eye on the bag of money. Mickey didn't say anything, but Steven could swear he saw Mickey wink his eye.

Several minutes later, Steven went back to the kitchen door. Steven's mother still had not opened the door. Steven knocked again. Eventually, Steven's mother opened the door, tying on her robe.

"Rio... Rio... Bur-bur-rito." Steven was asking for his chorizo burrito. That much made sense to Steven's mother.

"I'll put it in the microwave for you." She did.

"Here's your pill." She gave Steven the little, blue pill. Steven put it in his left pocket.

Steven's mother, Martha, spoke English. While it isn't her native tongue, she was born in the United States of America. She was born in Texas and learned English as quickly as she learned Spanish. Steven's father, Rogelio, met her there on his way to California in the mid Sixties. Rogelio met Martha at a local bar. She was only seventeen, lonely, and bored. Rogelio was twenty, and, really, just passing by. Maybe it was the liquor, but Rogelio thought she was the most beautiful woman he had ever seen. It was definitely the liquor that made Martha decide to have sex with him later that evening. Because Rogelio was on his way to California, he felt obligated after sex to ask her to come along with him. To his surprise, and slight disappointment, she said she would, and did. It was lucky for her that she did. Little did she know, minutes after her first sexual encounter with the man that would be her husband, they had conceived a child.

They didn't find out about the child until two months after it was conceived. By then, they had already had their civil ceremony and had established a rented garage in Boyle

Heights, California, in East Los Angeles, as their home.

The first child born was Rogelio Meresko, Junior. They called him Junior. Junior looked just like Rogelio Senior, without any resemblance to Martha. Had Junior not come out of Martha, they would have questioned whether she was his mother at all. Rogelio Senior loved Junior. He loved Junior more than any of his other children. He loved him more than their second child, Natasha, and their set of twins, Esteban and Boris. He loved him even after Junior joined a gang at the age of thirteen. He loved Junior so much that he hardly ever beat the shit out of Junior. There were other gangs and fellow gang members that did that for him. He loved Junior more after Junior was shot in the leg, which never healed properly. He loved Junior so much that he sent Junior to live in Jocotepec, Mexico, at the farm in the small town where Rogelio was raised, with hopes that Junior would get the gang mentality out of his head. It sort of worked. Only Junior started hanging out with one of his drunken uncles, drinking along with him. Junior made friends who would also drink. Junior couldn't count how many times, after being driven home by his uncle, he got home so drunk that he almost fell into the farm's well after vomiting into it. He told that to his friends a million times. "Shit, I don't know how many times I came home so drunk that I almost fell into the well," he said in Spanish, except for the word "shit," that was in English. They were a group of fourteen year olds, a sort of gang, if you will. Junior would borrow his uncle's car and drive around the town, shunning any traffic laws that only existed on paper, anyway. He would show off for the girls, for his friends, for anybody that was looking. One night, Junior had been drinking, as usual, but, unlike usual, Junior decided he wanted to go back to his grandmother's farm early, while his head was still relatively clear, after thinking about all of the close calls he had with the well. He asked his uncle to borrow the car. His uncle was so drunk he just handed Junior the keys without even considering how he would get himself home that night. At the time, Junior's uncle wasn't thinking about that. He just wanted more booze. Junior didn't consider how his uncle was going to get home, either. He just wanted to get himself home slightly less drunk than usual, if only to avoid any missteps that would lead him to a nosedive in the well. Junior figured that thinking about the well as he drove home would keep him a safe distance from the well when he got there, certainly avoiding that unfortunate accident. While his thinking of the well kept him from falling into the well, it didn't keep him from driving off the road. He was deep in thought about the well. He didn't see that his car was drifting. When he realized that he was about to strike a tree, his bum leg, where he had been shot, didn't react in time. There was shattered glass on the dirt around the tree, and some even reached the paved road. His crooked torso was only halfway out of the windshield, but only because the same tree that accordioned the car's hood, stopped his trajectory. The scene of the accident was so gory that a photograph of the mangled car, tree, and Junior's body made the cover of *Alarma*, a Mexican magazine that showcases acts of violence, stupidity, and accidents. Junior was dead. Steven's father was devastated when he heard about the accident. His uncle called with the news. A month later he called again and asked Rogelio if he wanted a copy of the latest *Alarma* magazine, showcasing Junior. Rogelio didn't want it. He wanted his son back, but knew that it would never happen. He kept himself sane with the knowledge that he had two more sons that he was certain he was going to mold into the son he always wished Junior would be. That was why he would beat them. He figured that enough abuse would keep his sons in line. He would leave his daughter's future in the hands of his wife.

Steven's family ended-up in Boyle Heights because Rogelio had a cousin, a plumber, who was living there, also in a garage, but on a different block. As devout Catholics, Rogelio, his family, and his cousin and his family would meet every Sunday at church. They went to a Church called *El Santuario de la Virgen de Guadalupe*, The Sanctuary of the Virgin of Guadalupe. Even after the family moved farther east, the family continued to attend the same church.

Steven didn't like going to that church because it was always crowded and the mass seemed to go on forever. He did, however, like the warm, steamy tamales and thick, sweet *champurrado* that he would get afterwards. Steven also liked the church carnival. Steven's parents didn't like the carnivals. The church carnivals didn't lend themselves well to that church. Parking was a nightmare on any given Sunday. Factor in the fact that the church held its carnival on the church parking lot, and you can see the escalated problem. The carnival even attracted people that didn't go to the church. It attracted local children, gangsters, and slutty teenage girls that were looking for the gangsters to help them make children. Still, the carnival generated a lot of money for the church, more so than the money collected in the collection plates. Then again, the church didn't expect much money in their collection plate because the attendees didn't have much money to spare as an offertory. They certainly did have money to spare on carnival activities.

The ceremony was in Spanish and, while Steven spoke Spanish as fluently as he spoke English—which is to say not very fluently, what with his stuttering after the accident—the priest used big Spanish words that Steven didn't understand. Steven didn't like that. He knew the prayers because he had them somewhat memorized, but he didn't know what they were saying. He particularly liked the "Act of Contrition." He liked how halfway through, as though choreographed, everybody said, *"Por mi culpa, por mi culpa, por mi gran culpa,"* and tapped their hearts with a closed fist in unison. Steven liked seeing his father do this. He was perfectly in sync with everybody else in the church. Steven was always off by a millisecond. He was off by more than a millisecond after the accident. In fact, Rogelio was also slightly off after Steven's accident. Steven noticed that after the accident Rogelio pressed his fist tighter, cringed his face, and hit, rather than tapped his heart. He also closed his eyes and sounded the words, rather than mouthed them, *"Por mi culpa, por mi culpa, por mi gran culpa."* Steven never knew why, but Rogelio did.

Steven knew that the mass was coming to an end when it was time to shake everybody's hands. While Steven was happy that the mass was practically over, he didn't like shaking people's hands. It made Steven uncomfortable, so usually he would purposefully bend down and tie his shoes during that part of the mass, so as to avoid any obligation.

Steven liked the drive home after church. He liked it mostly because he knew that he wouldn't have to go back to church for another week. He liked driving past all the cemeteries. Steven was always fascinated by a Jewish cemetery that they always drove past on their way home. He knew it was a Jewish cemetery because his father once told Steven, "See all of those graves. Those all belong to Jews." Steven found this fascinating because he was under the impression that Hitler had killed every single Jew in Germany. That was history as far as he understood it. He was retarded. Interestingly, the cemetery that Steven's father always pointed out to Steven wasn't, in fact, a Jewish cemetery. It was a Chinese cemetery. But Steven's father never bothered to do any research. Why should he? Forget the fact that there were Chinese characters written all around the cemetery. Those types of details were lost on Steven's father. Calling it a Jewish cemetery was enough to encompass any foreign people, for all intents and purposes.

Steven's mother would point out things to Steven while driving home, as well. She once pointed out a bunch of young girls dressed in tight, skimpy dresses that scooped really low on the neck, exposing a long crack of cleavage, and inched really high on the rump, exposing thick, meaty, pale thighs. They were walking across an intersection littered with broken glass. "Look at all those girls. My God. The way they're dressed, showing off everything. I bet they wouldn't get dressed like that to go to church," she said, pulling her shawl tighter around her shoulders. Steven looked at them, but hardly considered their appearance. Curiously, the provocatively dressed girls that Steven's mother criticized were actually on their way to church—to the church carnival.

But before Steven and his family could make their way home, Steven would have to suffer the awkwardness of the handshaking, even if it was just his parents' hands. He didn't even like to shake his father's hand. It felt weird when he felt his father's hand against his own. The only times he usually felt his father's hand was when it was crashing against his face and ass. Shaking it just seemed weird. Steven's father never offered it to him anyway, not after the accident. His mother didn't shake Steven's hand either. She hardly even looked at him anymore. Not when she handed him his little, blue pill, not when she told him that his burrito was in the microwave. Never.

    Bob looked at Steven. It was more like a stare than a look. Bob always stared at Steven. It made Steven uncomfortable. It made Steven feel as though Bob was scrutinizing the very depth of Steven, as though Bob was investigating a crime that had never been committed, looking for evidence within the chambers of Steven's heart, dusting for prints on his very soul. Steven felt as though Bob was waiting for him to make a mistake, or staring at Steven to try to find out some information, or something. Steven was suspicious of Bob's stares. As it were, Bob wouldn't stare at Steven for any of the reasons that Steven had speculated. Bob would stare at Steven to see if he could see any resemblance to Steven's mother. He couldn't.

    After handing Steven his burrito, Steven saw his mother walk back through the kitchen, and disappear into the dining room. As she rounded the corner that led to the living room, Steven heard her robe fall to the ground. Steven imagined that he could grab a knife from one of the kitchen drawers and do what he had to do right then and there. What Mickey had told him he had to do. He didn't. He figured the knives in the kitchen were not as effective as a knife he once saw in a movie. The movie was First Blood, starring Sylvester Stallone. Steven liked the movie because it was one of the last movies he saw in the theater. He went with his father to the Golden Gate Theater, in East Los Angeles, on Atlantic Boulevard to see First Blood. Nobody else wanted to go. After the movie, Rogelio asked Steven what the characters were saying to each other because the movie was in English, and Steven's father only spoke Spanish. Steven explained it as best as he could. Although he barely understood a word that Sylvester Stallone said, he managed. Steven's retelling changed the movie plot a bit, but the theme remained the same: a misunderstanding gone awry.

Steven wanted Rambo's knife. He knew where to get it. He knew that there was one place nearby that had anything anybody could possibly want: Kmart. Steven knew he had to go to Kmart and buy the Rambo knife. Before leaving, however, he had to go back to his garage to put the little, blue pill in his drawer and get his money. He did just that, with a burrito in hand, and walked along the driveway that would have led cars toward the garage that is now his room. He exited the iron gate with the twenty-four inch row of chicken wire along its base that was there to keep a dog that no longer lived from exiting the premises without permission.

Chapter VI

Steven's burrito was still too hot to eat. He has eaten hot burritos before and has burned the roof of his mouth to the point where the ridges on his palate closest to his front teeth felt engorged, and the farther back he'd slide his tongue, the more he imagined the roof of his mouth felt like a split ribcage. And, the constant prodding of his tongue on those inflamed ridges would eventually cause a flap of skin to hang from the roof of his mouth, on which Steven would fixate until he would attempt to reach into his mouth with fingers that were too thick to effectively tug at a small flap of skin that, to his tongue, felt like it should have been the size of an old-timey barber's razor strap, but, in fact, was mere millimeters long. Regardless, he didn't want this to happen again. Steven's mother allowed the burrito to heat for one minute and twenty seconds. She doesn't know that she is overheating the food because she wouldn't dare eat a burrito that she has microwaved. She wouldn't dare, because she doesn't have to. She insists on fresh food whether it's served by an old waitress, delivered by a young driver, or cooked by a naked woman. She insists that her food is freshly prepared. She says, "Thank you Jesus Christ, my Lord and Savior for these hot provisions." But by "hot" she means immediate, not nuked. Steven has, by trial and error, learned to manage microwave heat. But, sometimes, he forgets because he just wants to eat. When he forgets, he starts back upon biting, letting whatever hasn't stuck to those throbbing ridges on the roof of his mouth rain down to the floor in spicy chunks, along with a web of saliva that had prepped his mouth in anticipation of said bite. Steven has tried to tell his mother on separate occasions.

"No . . . No, no, no. No. I . . . No." Those were the words that came out of his mouth. Steven was even fanning his mouth with his left hand. Steven's mother could not make any sense of Steven's words. She tried, as usual, anyway.

"It's not too spicy. Just eat it. Praise the Lord for the food that you eat."

Such was the case this time. Steven stood on the sidewalk in front of his house for several minutes. He was waiting for his burrito to cool. He held the burrito up toward the sun to see if there was any steam emanating from the bite. His focus shifted from the would-be steam toward a person several yards away. He saw his neighbor from down the street, Tony Chafas. Tony Chafas was walking to work at the liquor store down the street that his family owned. Steven ran toward Tony, burrito in hand like a dented baton. Tony continued walking, smoking a cigarette. Steven walked beside him.

"Washa. Washa. Wah . . . Wah. Washa. I wanna . . . Wanna." Tony didn't know what Steven was saying.

"Really?"

"Washa. Washa. Wa. Wanna."

"Yeah? When?"

"Washa. Washa. I wanna . . . Wanna."

"Really?"

"Washa. Wanna."

"Okay."

Tony was pretending as though he had a clue as to what Steven was saying. Steven fell for it because, by chance, what

Tony had responded coincided with what Steven was trying to say. Had Steven's speech been articulate, the conversation would have gone like this:

"I'm going to kill my mother. She wants to take my bottle collection."

"Really?"

"Mickey told me. She's planning it right now. I have to kill her."

"Yeah? When?"

"Today. I'm going to Kmart to buy a knife."

"Really?"

"Yes. I have no choice."

"Okay."

Steven liked Tony Chafas. They went to school together. They were never friends, at least not according to Tony. Steven always considered Tony a friend even after Tony announced to their kindergarten class that Steven had pissed his pants, and after putting up with the twigs and cigarette buts that Tony put up Steven's ass. Steven always felt that Tony understood him. They had conversations. Tony listened to Steven. That was what Steven thought.

"I have to go now, Steven. My dad has to come home for lunch."

"Washa."

"Yeah. I'll see you later."

Tony continued walking and smoking. Tony had to go relieve his father behind the counter at Art's Liquor. Steven was a regular at Art's Liquor. He never bought any liquor, though. Steven would go to Art's Liquor every other day to buy himself a Snickers bar. The Snickers bar supplemented his diet, sustaining his energy plenty long enough until his next burrito. Yeah, they really satisfied him.

Steven stopped in front of a neighbor's house. There was a Chihuahua behind a chain-link fence that Steven has been teasing since it was a puppy. The Chihuahua barked and barked every time Steven walked by. Steven liked to run back and forth in front of the fence and liked watching the dog follow him, barking at his feet. He sometimes stopped and batted the fence with his hands and kicked it with his feet. The dog's owner, a middle-aged, unemployed man named Albert, would eventually come out of the house and yell at Steven.

"Leave my dog alone you fucking retard!" Then he mumbled to himself, "you slow-brained motherfucker," so as to not insult Steven.

Whenever this happened, Steven would run away, so as to avoid more confrontation.

Strangely, the owner didn't only call Steven a retard. He also called his Chihuahua, Baby, a retard. He also called Baby a stupid dog, mangy mutt, stupid bitch, *pinche perra pendeja*. He called Baby a retard one night when she was sleeping on his lap as he watched television. All of the sudden, Baby began twitching. She even let out a tiny yelp. Then she stopped twitching and continued with her sleep. Seeing this, Albert asked the dog, "What are you, retarded?" Naturally, the dog didn't reply, nor did Albert really expect a reply. He just asked for the sake of asking. What Albert didn't know was that the reason Baby twitched and let out a little yelp was because she was having a dream that she saw feet running back and forth in front of the chain-link fence, and she was chasing them, the way she did almost everyday.

Ironically, Albert was retarded, by definition, anyway. That is, he is retarded according to his ex-boss, a plumbing contractor. He had sent Albert on a job where he was to fix a leak. When Albert arrived at the residence, he was greeted by a fat, old man that he swears looked like Santa Claus, were it not for two brown streaks that were below his nostrils on his otherwise white facial hair. The brown streaks existed on account of the fat, old man's smoking habit. The fat, old man had seen a trickle of mud near the opening to the crawl space beneath the house. After shining a flash light into the crawl space and seeing a steady trickle of water falling from a pipe, he thought to himself, "No fucking way am I going down there to fix that shit." So, when Albert got there, the fat, old man told Albert, jokingly, "No fucking way am I going down there to fix that shit." Only, not really jokingly. Either way, Albert was going to crawl under the house. It was his job, after all.

Albert crawled under the house and saw that the problem was due to a deteriorated section of cast iron pipe. It was to be a simple procedure. Still, Albert felt compelled to tell the fat, old man that he had a serious plumbing problem, that he would have to spend most of the day under the house and that it would cost a pretty penny. Albert said, "It's pretty serious. I'll probably spend the entire day under there. It's going to cost you a pretty penny." Albert offered to show the fat, old man the problem, knowing full well that the fat, old man would never be able to get under the house due to his fatness and oldness. Besides, the fat, old man had already made it pretty clear that he wouldn't be going down there.

The fat, old man, thinking he didn't have any options, told Albert to do whatever he had to do. Albert did. It took him just over forty minutes to saw off the section of corroded cast-iron pipe and replace it with another piece which he attached with a couple of couplings. The rest of the time, Albert stayed under the house smoking cigarettes. Occasionally, Albert turned on his reciprocal saw and banged on the pipes with his wrench to make it sound as though he was actually doing something. He even took several breaks in between. The fat, old man came by every couple of hours with ice water. Albert was loving it.

That evening, he returned to his boss's office and turned in his time card, which had an explanation of his work. His boss couldn't believe that it took him six hours to do the job. He asked Albert, "Six hours? What did you do?"

"It was this fat, old man that looked like Santa Claus. His name was Nick. He just had a leak under the house. I fixed it."

"It took you six hours?"

"No. I was done in like forty minutes. C'mon, any retard could fix that in no time at all. I just stayed under the house and smoked cigarettes. Fuck it. We made a shit load of money."

"What are you, retarded?"

Albert never got to answer the question. He was asked to leave and never to return. He didn't. He stayed home, and hardly ever left. That is until a couple of days before Steven decided to kill his mother.

On the day that Steven decided to kill his mother, Steven didn't tease Baby. He stopped in front of the fence and took a couple of bites of his burrito. Baby saw that Steven was eating and so it stood on its hind legs, it bulbous eyes threatening to pop out of its head. Steven figured that the dog must be hungry, because, for once, it wasn't barking, so he tossed it a bit that he tore off of his burrito. Steven took a couple more bites in between feeding Baby little slivers of greasy tortilla. Eventually, Steven gave the rest of the burrito to Baby, the end part with the multiple layers of tortilla folded upon each other cupping the fattiest chunks of pork, and grease-soaked potato and egg. That was lucky for Baby because she hadn't eaten in two days. Albert had gone to Las Vegas because his wife stopped coming home. She couldn't stand the pathetic, unemployed man that Albert had become. He hadn't seen or heard from his wife and daughter in two months. Albert had decided to go to Las Vegas, not to gamble—he didn't have any money; he hadn't worked in nearly a year—but to look for his wife. He didn't have any reason to believe that she had gone to Las Vegas. It was just an arbitrary place where he figured he would start looking for her. He spent the entire day walking around the Las Vegas Strip, staring at people's faces and would feel his heart sink whenever he saw the back of a woman's head that resembled his wife's. He didn't find her there. That night, he found a really cheap motel where he decided he would hang himself. He did. Ironically, his wife and daughter were living in an unfurnished apartment, not in Las Vegas, but just two blocks away from Albert's own home, across the street from Art's Liquor.

    Steven didn't know any of this had gone on, nor did he care. He liked seeing Baby eat the burrito, only he didn't know that Baby was named Baby. Steven called him *Chiquito*, after his own Chihuahua, because Steven didn't know what else to call it. Steven also didn't know that within two weeks, Baby would be lying on the warm cement of Albert's back yard, twitching. Only the twitching wouldn't be due to a dream of chasing feet running back and forth in front of the chain-link fence, but rather of Baby's body giving up on living due to a lack of food and water.

Chapter VII

After feeding Baby the burrito, Steven began walking to Kmart. He walks everywhere—limps, rather. That is why Steven is so skinny. At one point, Steven weighed nearly three hundred pounds. He was fat for most of his life. He didn't always weigh three hundred pounds, but he always weighed more than was considered healthy by health professionals. Steven didn't care that he was fat. He didn't care that, along with "retard," everybody called him fat-ass, fatty, chunk, tubby, lardo, *tonona, gordo, panzón, barrigón*. He didn't care that everybody told him "goddamn, you're fat," "fucking fat-ass," and *"sigue cenando."* By everybody, I mean his parents, siblings, friends, neighbors, teachers, business owners, passers-by—just about everybody that Steven has known, met, seen, or heard of him. Steven didn't know that so many people were making fun of his weight. He only knew of a few. He didn't care that those few made fun of his weight. He cared even less if anybody else makes fun of his weight. Now, his weight isn't an issue. He's down to one hundred seventy-five pounds. He didn't go on any Subway, protein, or bullshit Paleo diet. His weight loss was due to his walking everywhere, all the time.

Steven has to walk everywhere. He can't drive, and he would rather save on bus fare, since he has very little money to begin with. Because he has to walk everywhere, Steven's mother had to invest money on some quality walking shoes. By quality, she meant cheap. By walking shoes, she meant any pair of shoes that were cheap. Steven's mother noticed Steven's need for new shoes five years ago when she saw him walking and noticed that the soles of his Converse All Stars—which she got on sale for $19.99—were falling off, hanging like tongues with every step, slapping the bottoms of Steven's feet.

Steven's mother decided to give Steven forty dollars. She told him, "Here's forty dollars. Buy yourself some quality walking shoes. Buy a bag of socks and a sweatshirt and bring back the change. Don't buy anything else. Christ be with you." Christ would have to be standing right next to Steven if he was going to walk out of a shoe store with a pair of quality walking shoes, a bag of socks, a sweatshirt, and still come home with change.

Steven didn't question it. He took the money and walked to a shoe store on Atlantic Boulevard, in East Los Angles, called Athletic Shoe World. Steven had seen it before, on his way home from church, back when his father was still alive. While there were plenty of other shoe stores nearby, Steven wanted to go to Athletic Shoe World because he imagined, by the name alone, that it must be enormous.

It took Steven nearly an hour and a half to walk to Athletic Shoe World. Once he arrived, he noticed a sign out front that read, "Shoes: Two pares for $40." Steven didn't consider the poor spelling and grammar. He was interested in getting some shoes, the quality kind.

To Steven's surprise, he walked in to find his neighbor, Tony Chafas, working in the store. This was back before Art's Liquor. Tony wasn't actually working. He was sitting behind the counter watching the NFL All-Star football game, getting paid, nonetheless. What Steven didn't know was that later that day, Athletic Shoe World would get robbed, and his friend Tony Chafas would quit his job. But that didn't matter. What mattered was that Steven was about to get some shoes.

"Sh . . . Sh . . . Shoe." What Steven was trying to tell Tony was that he wanted two pair of shoes for forty dollars. Luckily, Steven was pointing outside at the sign, so Tony caught his drift.

"Nah. You don't want those shoes. They're no good. These are good shoes." Tony got up off his chair, walked from behind the counter toward a series of shelves lined with single shoes tightly wrapped in plastic, and handed Steven a pair of shoes that cost more than forty dollars, three times more.

"Sh . . . Sh . . . Shoe," Steven said again, pointing again.

Tony wasn't going to pressure Steven into buying the more expensive shoe, even if it was costing Tony one dollar in sales commission. He would give Steven what he wanted.

"Okay. These are the shoes that are two for forty. They're L. A. Gears. They come with the gray trim and the pink trim."

"Yeah . . . Yah . . . Yeah," Steven said, pointing at the shoes with gray trim.

"Okay. What size?"

"I oh, I oh, I oh. I oh . . . I oh no." Steven threw up his hands and shook his head.

"Let me see. Take off your shoe." This proved to be one of the biggest mistakes in Tony's life. Just as Steven took off his shoe, right when the heel of the shoe was coming off of his foot, Tony nearly vomited. The smell was unlike any smell that Tony had ever experienced. Had Tony vomited, it would have made the area smell nicer. That's how bad it was. The shoes were, after all, five years old. He did walk everywhere, and he hardly every changed his socks. There's really no wonder. You'd think that the fact that the shoes were practically falling apart, that this would allow his feet to air out a bit. But, no. This actually allowed more moisture to enter from wet grass and puddles and what not increasing the dank.

Steven didn't notice. He just looked under the shoes tongue and held the shoe up to Tony, this time throwing up only one hand. "I oh, I oh, I oh. I oh . . . I oh no."

"Just look at the bottom of your shoe. Converse All-Stars have the size at the bottom of the sole." While this was true, Steven's sole was so worn down, that the size was shaved off by use years ago. Tony realized that the size no longer existed when Steven showed him the bottom of his shoe. Tony had two options: take out that metal contraption that was behind the counter and measure Steven's feet, or bring out several boxes of shoes and let Steven search for the right size. Naturally, Tony opted for the latter. He didn't know how to use that metal thing anyway.

Steven eventually found his size. He was a size eleven. Tony brought out a second pair and took both to the counter.

Steven stopped Tony. "I wah . . . I wah." Steven was telling Tony that he was going to wear a pair home. Steven put the pair on and spent twenty minutes lacing them up. He then handed Tony his stinky pair of Converse All-Stars. Tony didn't take them. He held out a plastic bag and had Steven place the shoes in there. Tony quickly tied the plastic bag and threw it in the trash. Tony imagined that the plastic bag might begin to fill with the foul gases that the shoes were emitting, and that the bag might explode. He stopped thinking that when Steven got his attention.

"Anything else?"

"So-so . . . So-so . . . So-so." Steven was asking for a bag of socks. He pointed at them. Tony got them.

"Okay. That's $51.03."

Steven handed Tony forty dollars. Tony looked at Steven, rolled his eyes, and shook his head pitifully. Tony handed Steven the bag with the shoes and socks. Steven extended his hand, "Sh . . . Sha-sha . . . Sha." Steven was asking for change. Tony didn't realize this.

Tony grabbed Steven's hand and shook it. "You're welcome. I'll see you."

Steven walked out of Athletic Shoe World wearing a new pair of shoes, carrying a bag with another new pair and bag of socks, and walked home. It took him longer to get home. Not because he was getting used to his new shoes, nor because of his limp. It took him longer to get home because he was crying, and he kept stopping because it was hard for Steven to cry and walk. He was sobbing because he knew that his mother was going to get mad at him because he didn't bring home any change. When he got home, his mother did get mad at him. Had it been his father, Steven would have gotten the beating of a lifetime. But, his father was dead. His mother could be just as abusive when she was mad. She was mad at the fact that he bought two pair of shoes, rather than one, he didn't buy his sweater, and he didn't bring home any change. "Jesus Christ, help my son understand. He isn't right. Help me my Lord, Jesus Christ, Heavenly Father and Savior."

Steven soon got over it. He had two pair of shoes. So

far, they have lasted him five years. One pair has, anyway. The first pair nearly fell apart nearly three years ago. He could have continued wearing the pair for a few more months, but given the fact that he had a brand new pair in the waiting, he opted for new rather than old. The second pair has lasted slightly longer because two years ago, Steven got a bike, though he didn't have it for very long.

He bought it at a yard sale that he found one day while walking around. Only Steven didn't buy it on the day of the yard sale. He saw it on the driveway and told the old, fat man with a white beard and mustache streaked brown at the nostrils who was selling it, "Bah-bah. Bah-bah. Bah-bah-bike." The old, fat man's name was Nick, one of the many neighborhood drunks. Steven considered Nick, like Tony, a friend. Steven called him Santa because Nick looked like Santa. Clever.

"Hey, Steven. You like that bike?"

"Yah. Yah-yah. Yah."

"I'll give it to you for fifteen dollars. I don't need it anymore. Some fuck-wad, asshole, piece of shit hit me with his car when I was riding that bike. Nearly killed me." It was a rusty, old, brown Schwinn. It was barely worth the fifteen dollars, but Steven didn't have the money.

"Rah. Rah." Steven was trying to say that he would be back in a few weeks with the money. Then he left. Nick thought Steven was telling him that he would be right back with the money, so he put it aside and didn't sell it, even though several people inquired about it.

"Sorry folks, this baby is spoken for," he would say when anybody asked.

Most people weren't too disappointed. "Piece of shit, anyway," they would say to themselves.

It took Steven three weeks to save-up for the bike. He eventually went back to Nick's house and handed him a sandwich bag filled with coins and several dollars. At first, Nick didn't know what was going on. He was a drunk. He could hardly remember what he did ten minutes ago. Then, with a snap of his fingers, he remembered the bike, and he rolled it out of the garage. Nick didn't bother to count the money. Neither did Steven. Had either bothered to count it, they would have noticed that Steven had over-paid by $2.15. Either way, Steven had a bike, and Nick went to Art's Liquor and celebrated the sale with two forty-ounce bottles of Lazer Malt Liquor. Everybody wins.

It took Steven a few weeks to get the hang of riding a bike. When he first brought it home, Steven's mother questioned where he got it. "Where did you get that thing? Did you steal it? Jesus Christ, forgive my son for he knows not what he does."

"Bah-bah. Bah-bah. Bah-bah-bike. Nah-nah-nick."

Steven's mother didn't know what he said. She figured she had already asked Jesus Christ for forgiveness, and that was pretty much all she could do.

For the first week, Steven just walked around the neighborhood pulling the bike along side of him. Eventually, he sat on the seat and just pushed himself with the toes of his feet, as though he was walking. When he finally mustered the nerve to place his feet on the pedals, he wobbled and turned, but he stayed on. He would put his feet down just before he was going to fall. He fell a few times, but it didn't hurt much. He still cried, though.

Once, he saw a couple of neighborhood kids riding their bikes. Steven decided he would follow them. The kids noticed that Steven was riding toward them, so they sped-up and bunny-hopped their way onto the sidewalk. Steven had never bunny-hopped onto the sidewalk. Whenever he wanted to get onto the sidewalk, he went up a driveway, a wheelchair ramp, or got off of his bike and carried it onto the sidewalk. But Steven was determined to follow them, which he did, for a few seconds. Steven hardly even attempted to bunny-hop onto the sidewalk. He rode directly into the curb, pulling at his handlebars, thinking that his rubber tires would pop him up and onto the sidewalk, which they did, only his bike stayed on the street. Steven cried as the boys he was following rode away laughing.

That was when Steven decided he would return the bike to Nick.

"Bah-bah. Bah-rah. Bah-rah-bike." Steven was asking for his money back.

"What? What do you want, Steven?"

"Bah-bah. Bah-rah. Bah-rah-bike." Steven extended his hand and tapped the center of his palm.

"I'm not giving you your money back. You've had the bike for months. What do you think, I'm retarded?"

"Fuh-fuh-fuck. Fuck. Fuck. Fuh-fuh-fuck." Steven threw the bike to the ground and walked home, crying. He was upset. He eventually got over it.

By the following weekend, Nick had painted the rusty bike's frame red with an old can of spray paint. The rust on the bike caused the paint to dimple, creating a texture on the frame similar to painted sandpaper. Regardless, he sold the bike the following weekend at his yard sale for forty dollars, and what remained of the can of red spray paint for a quarter. Once again, Nick celebrated by going to Art's Liquor and buying two forty-ounce bottles of Lazer Malt Liquor.

    Steven didn't know, nor did he care about what had happened to his bike. He was fine with walking. He enjoyed it. His L. A. Gear shoes, with their gray trim, were getting him where he wanted to go. At the moment, he was on his way to Kmart.

Chapter VIII

Steven's twin brother, Boris, also had L. A. Gear shoes. Only Boris's L. A. Gear shoes had the pink trim. Boris was gay. Like Steven, Boris had always been fat. Also like Steven, Boris lost a lot of weight. Unlike Steven, Boris didn't lose his weight by walking around a lot. He lost his weight because he had an affinity for ecstasy and he contracted AIDS.

He was an actor, or so he said. He actually bagged groceries at a Pavilions in West Hollywood, where he shared a studio apartment with four other gay men. Like Steven, he no longer went by the name he was born with. Boris Meresko was now known as Robert Nealen. Bob, if you will. While the name fit his extracurricular activities, it didn't fit his appearance. Boris's face was undoubtedly Mexican. He looked so native that if he told people that he helped build the Mayan pyramids of Chichen Itza, they would believe him. What made things more bizarre was the fact that Bob spoke with a British accent. Nobody knows how that came about. Not even Bob. While it didn't happen over night, it has since gotten so Cockneyed that his speech is almost as incomprehensible as Steven's.

Bob also had severely limp wrists. Had a trawling physician seen Bob walking along the streets of West Hollywood, that physician would have wondered if Bob had ever damaged his radial nerves. His wrists were that limp. The fact was that Bob, back when he was still Boris, had damaged his radial nerves, only not so severely that his wrists would continue to dangle so limply. This dangling was more aesthetic than anything. He damaged his radial nerves one day when he and Steven were playing "Star Wars." Their game had hardly anything to do with the plot of Star Wars, as much as it only had to do with the names of the characters in Star Wars. Their game of Star Wars consisted of Steven and Boris jumping off of the bed of their father's truck yelling, "Chewbacca," "Yoda," Stormtrooper!" Once, with more than usual elevation, Boris yelled, "Princess Leia!" His chunky legs gave way upon landing, forcing his wrists to take the brunt of his heavy weight. His wrists hurt him for days after that, but he never went to the hospital. His wrists eventually healed, mostly. But, he still walks with his wrists dangling before him like the front paws of a dog walking on its hind legs.

Bob left home the day after the death of his father. He didn't tell anybody where he was going. He just left. He left behind a note for his mother. All the note said was, "I'm gay." No salutation, no closing. Just those two words.

At first, his mother wasn't quite sure what to make of the note. She figured it out within minutes. He called her a few months later to give her his phone number. He left a message on the answering machine. But, his mother never returned the call. She couldn't get over the fact that he was gay, although she always knew. So did Steven's father, although he never mentioned it. All Steven's mother could say after reading the note was, "Jesus Christ, Heavenly Father and Savior, cure my son of his evil ways," to no avail.

The only thing Bob was ever cured of was his profound desire to stick foreign objects in his ass. He loved it. He stuck fruit, vegetables, toothbrushes, hairbrushes, bar soap, dildos, vibrators. He once stuck a champagne bottle in his ass after a night of drinking. He came home alone one night after bagging groceries. He brought with him a three-dollar bottle of champagne. His roommates were out, so he drank the bottle by himself. Be it loneliness or drunkenness, soon, his desires took over. He saw the empty bottle of champagne and figured it would feel fantastic inside of him. While he enjoyed the initial penetration and the feeling of the bottle slowly sliding into him, and feeling it hang a little as he walked around the house with the bottle in his ass, he didn't like the feeling he got when he attempted to pull the bottle out. What happened was the bottle had formed a vacuum, so that every time he attempted to pull the bottle out, the bottle sucked at his rectum, threatening to swallow it up. Bob realized this when he gave it a good tug. He began to panic. He didn't know what to do.

Bob called his friend Ruben and explained his dilemma. Bob was amazed that Ruben was at home because as long as Bob has known him, Ruben was always out on the town. Ruben was known around town as the good-time-go-to-guy. He always seemed to have a date. Ruben explained to Bob about the vacuum within the bottle inside his ass, and told Bob that he knew exactly what had to be done because it had happened to him several years ago, only it had happened with a bottle of Courvoisier. Ruben told Bob that he had to drill a hole at the base of the champagne bottle in order to release the vacuum. Bob would then be able to slide the bottle right out.

"I say, do ya ave a drull," he asked, as British as the Queen of England.

"Yes. I'll be right over."

Ruben came right over and drilled the base of the bottle, just as he had said had to be done. Bob enjoyed the sensation of the vibrating bottle, and then the feel of the bottle sliding right out. Bob was never happier. He thanked Ruben and kissed him until they were both on the floor naked. That night would be the last time Bob ever stuck any non-human foreign object in his ass. That night would also be the night that Bob contracted HIV, which would eventually lead to Bob's AIDS.

Soon after, Bob had become very depressed. His sex life, which up until then was rampant, had disappeared. He never wanted to do anything. He figured that before he died he would get the sex change operation that he always felt he needed. He wanted the sex change operation for as long as he could remember. Since he wasn't doing anything with his grocery-bagging money besides splitting rent, he figured that he would save it until he had enough to make himself the woman that he always knew he actually was. His friend Ruben had told him about a man in Tijuana that would perform the operation for super cheap. Ruben said, "There's this man in Tijuana—he's American—who will do the operation for, like, super cheap. He can do anything, and he charges hardly anything. Like, six thousand, or something. A few of my boyfriends told me about him. Everybody knows that doc. He's, like, famous, or something." While six thousand dollars was cheap, it was a lot for a guy that bagged groceries. Bob was determined to save his money, but that eventually changed. Eventually, Bob discovered ecstasy. That little pill changed Bob's life, and the life of many others that met Bob while he was on ecstasy. Bob was back in action and didn't slow down for several years. His weight decreased, at first, due to the ecstasy. Soon AIDS had settled. Now, he is on his way out.

Steven knows that his twin brother is gay. He doesn't know that he changed his name to Bob, that he is dying of AIDS, nor that he speaks in a British accent. Steven's mother told him, "Your brother is gay. Jesus Christ, help him."

In a way, Steven had always known that his brother was gay. He heard the neighborhood kids tease Boris. "Boris the fag," they would call him. They would tell Steven, "Hey retard, where's your faggot brother?" Steven was just a kid. He didn't know how to answer that. They would also ask, "When did you find out your brother was a fag?" Again, Steven didn't know how to answer that. So, he didn't. He would just walk away. "I asked you a question, retard." Steven ignored them, but he would eventually curse his gay brother, "Fug . . . Fug . . . Fuh-Fug . . . Fuh-fuh-Fug . . . Fuckin' faggot." While Steven didn't care so much that his brother was gay, he did care that his mother liked Boris more than she liked Steven. Steven had always been a daddy's boy, while Boris was a momma's boy. It just turned out that way.

Steven, certainly, was not gay. As a young boy, he liked a girl that lived next door to him, back when Steven's family lived in Boyle Heights. Her name was Felicia. Once, Steven saw her vagina. She was playing with her dolls in her back yard with Steven's brother, Boris. Steven was in his own back yard when Steven's father asked Steven to get his brother for dinner. Of course, Steven did what his father asked, right away. He had to, or he would surely suffer the consequences.

When he went to Felicia's back yard, he saw that Felicia had lifted her dress and was getting ready to urinate onto the dirt floor. Boris was sitting nearby surrounded by dolls. While Steven saw Felicia's vagina, it looked merely like a fold in her skin. Steven didn't think much of it. But he knew that he liked Felicia.

He also liked Felicia's dog, Snoopy. It was a little, puffy, white mutt with curly fur, a black nose, and a red collar. Felicia named the dog after her father, Snoopy, who was doing life in prison for the murder of a rival gang member. Steven didn't know the dog was named after Felicia's father, nor did Steven know that Felicia's father was in prison. Steven would play with Felicia's dog while Boris would play with Felicia and her dolls. It was a friendly dog. Steven liked that. He would sit on the dirt floor and hold the dog over his head, and hug it as though he were wrestling with it, playfully. This playfulness was unbeknownst to Snoopy. Eventually, the dog got tired of being manhandled. The dog bit Steven just below the eye. The bite left a clean gash with very little bleeding, yet deep enough to expose the thick layer of yellow fat in Steven's chunky face. The dog didn't know any better. Steven didn't care. He ran home and showed his mother what had happened. His mother told his father.

That same night, after beating the shit out of Steven for allowing the dog so near to his face, Steven's father went to Felicia's house, marched right into the yard, and grabbed the dog. When the dog saw Steven's father, the dog wagged its tail and licked its jowls with thoughts that it was about to be played with or given a treat. Steven's father didn't play with the dog nor give it a treat. Instead, he put the dog in the back of his truck and drove it a few miles east. He stopped the truck, got out, opened the truck's gate, and watched Snoopy dash out, and run away. Steven's father didn't see Snoopy get hit by a lunch truck several minutes later. The lunch truck's driver didn't see Snoopy, either. In fact, nobody saw Snoopy's dirty, bloody body twitching as it took its final breaths. What Steven's father did see was a house for sale as he drove home after releasing Snoopy, just a block away from Snoopy's carcass. He would eventually bring his family to live in that house. Steven eventually forgot about Felicia.

But he didn't stop liking females. However, there were no females that he particularly liked. He just liked to masturbate as a kid with the image of just about any woman that he saw on television. He learned how to masturbate at ten years old when he went to summer camp. He also learned how to make lanyards and *ojos de Dios* out of Popsicle sticks and colored yarn. The duration that he spent at camp was hardly the entire summer. It was only a week. Nobody complained because it was free. It was offered by a church that Steven's family didn't attend. Steven and Boris attended the camp, anyway. The camp was called Camp Saint Vincent de Paul. It was an all-boy's camp in the Malibu Mountains. Steven not only learned how to masturbate, make lanyards, and *ojos de Dios*, he also learned a song that he still sings when he's walking around. It goes:

> When a Camp Saint Vincent boy walks down the street,
> He looks one hundred percent perfect from head to feet.
> And if you look at him it's quite a treat,
> Hard to beat,
> A Camp Saint Vincent bo-o-oy.

Steven's brother Boris, or Bob, also sang the song when he used to walk around in his own neighborhood, only it was sung in a British accent.

Since they had to spend an entire week at summer camp, they were forced to bathe in a communal shower. This made Steven nervous. He had never seen so many naked people before. He eventually got used to it. It was in the shower that an older, black kid, Julius, told Steven, and any other kid that was listening, what "jacking-off" was. He told the kids that he stroked his penis and that it felt nice. He also said that it eventually ejaculated and that it felt good. Only Julius didn't say it quite like that. He said, "I grab my fucking dick, man, and I just yank it, man. I yank it and it gets all fucking hard and shit. I keep pulling at the motherfucker and pulling at it. It feels so fucking good. I start going faster and faster until—bam—all kinds of white shit flies out, all over the fucking place." Steven listened and laughed at the cuss words. When he went back home, he tried it. Sure enough, "Bam!" Boris also learned how to masturbate while listening to the conversations in the communal shower. That was also where Boris learned that he was gay.

Steven no longer masturbates. He never even considers masturbating. He has more important things to do. He gets his pleasure from collecting bottles, and that pleasure far outweighs any other. In fact, he decided that he would go to the Seven-Eleven dumpster to look for some bottles before he made his way to Kmart. He had time. He always had time for his collection.

Chapter IX

Steven's sister, Natasha, also collects things. However, unlike Steven, she still masturbates. Natasha is not retarded. She is fat. Some might say she is incredibly fat, and some do. Other's say she's huge, gigantic, a fat-ass, a fat bitch, a big mama, gigantor, *gordota, obesa.* Natasha doesn't know that so many people call her names. She hasn't left the house in seven years. She has hardly left her bed in five years. When she would leave the house, she heard a few people whisper things about her. That was back when she was a slender three hundred fifty pounds. Now that she weighs seven hundred pounds, ironically, Natasha has become invisible.

Natasha spends her days in bed watching television, eating, sleeping, masturbating, and recording radio shows on a tape recorder she brought from home. She left her home, like Steven's brother Boris, soon after the death of their father. Natasha was named Natasha due to the fact that her father could not let go of the smidgen of Russian that existed in his DNA. Natasha never liked her name. She would have preferred to have been named Rebecca, which, unbeknownst to Natasha, was on her father's short-list of names for her. Only her name would have been the Russian derivative of Rebecca, which is Revekka. He had to keep it Russian.

Natasha didn't run away, like Boris. She was already eighteen. She had plans to attend the University of California at Humboldt, in Northern California. She received financial aid on account of her low-income family. Financial Aid allowed

Natasha to get a small apartment in Eureka, just a few miles south of Arcata, the town in which the University was located. She would wake-up early and take the bus to school. Her plans were to study oceanography. She chose oceanography because she has always been fascinated and terrified of the ocean. She was fascinated by the fact that the ocean was self-sustaining, constant, and was home to a world that she could never be a part of. She was terrified of the ocean for the same reasons. While her intentions were to study, she never got around to doing too much of it. Because Natasha had always been overweight—however, not to the extent to which she is now—Natasha was made fun of in college. Her choice of study lent itself to a barrage of insults. One insult, in particular, which was made soon after deciding upon a major to declare, sent Natasha away from college forever: "You want to study the whales? Look in the mirror."

Her only response: "You're retarded." But she never went back to school.

Natasha never told her mother that she dropped out of school. She called her mother once and told her that she didn't know if school was really for her. She tried to explain to her mother that she was struggling a bit and was lonely. While all that was true, Natasha never mentioned to her mother that she hadn't been anywhere near the campus in six months. All her mother could say was, "Don't worry. With the help of Jesus Christ, our Savior, we can do anything." That didn't inspire Natasha to go back to school. The only time Natasha ever spoke to her mother again was when she called her mother for the phone number of her brother, Boris. Her mother gave Natasha Boris' number, but warned her that she had never called, so she didn't know if he still lived there. Natasha eventually called anyway. To her surprise, an English gentleman named Bob answered the phone. More surprising to Natasha was the fact that the English gentleman was Boris. After the initial shock, Natasha told Boris that she was miserable because she was so fat. Boris suggested a simple stomach stapling procedure, since, apparently, a diet and exercise were out of the question. She said she would certainly consider the procedure, but that it sounded expensive. Boris suggested a man in Tijuana who could do the operation for super cheap. Because of the relativity of the term "super cheap," and because of the proximity of Tijuana, Mexico, to Eureka, California, Natasha decided against the stomach stapling. She decided that being fat for the rest of her life was the most convenient thing to do. She never even spoke to her brother again. She wouldn't go back to school, either.

Instead of going back to school, she decided she would have a baby. The only problem was that she wasn't married, she didn't have a boyfriend, she has never had a boyfriend, and she weighed three hundred fifty pounds and counting. So there was more than one problem.

As luck would have it, Natasha lived down the street from a bar: *Jefe*'s. On some nights, *Jefe*'s is a hip hang-out that showcases local and traveling punk rock bands. On the night that Natasha decided to leave the house, *Jefe*'s was showcasing Mexican *Norteño* music. Natasha didn't arrive until very late at night. It was 1 am. The place would close in an hour. Natasha had planned on leaving her apartment earlier, but she had to get ready, and, because she had never gotten ready for anything like that, it took her quite a long time. Had you seen her, you wouldn't have guessed that it took her so long. Imagine a fat, Mexican woman with caked on make-up, applied as wobbly as her gait. That was Natasha that night. She didn't wear any underwear because she had heard about panty-lines, and she draped herself with a muumuu with hopes that it would accentuate her figure. Boy, did it accentuate her figure. And, no panty lines. She had decided that she was going to find herself a man.

She chose the right time and night to attend. All the men in the place were drunk. The women who were there were also drunk, but were swarmed upon the minute they entered the door. The men knew that the females there were there to dance closely and drink plenty. The men wanted the same, with hopes that the closeness of the dancing and the loads of booze would create the right spark that would ensure one less lonely night. All the men knew they had to move quickly. There was a sense of desperation so thick on the men in the room that you would swear they were ready to jump on each other. Men were singing along to the *ranchero* tunes, stumbling as they lifted their beers and liquors and took long swigs. They all sang particularly loud and with much intensity to a song by Ramon Ayala that went:

> *El día que yo me muera,*
> *No voy a llevarme nada.*
> *Hay que darle justo al gusto.*
> *La vida pronto se acaba.*
> *Lo que pasó en este mundo,*
> *No mas el recuerdo queda.*
> *Ya muerto voy a llevarme*
> *No mas un puño de tierra.*

When Natasha walked in, every desperate man in the room looked toward her. The sight of Natasha gave the men conflicting feelings within them. They didn't know what it was. Some questioned whether they may be drinking too much. Others wondered if they were gay. Some considered returning to Mexico. One man, Miguel, who was standing by the door, grabbed Natasha's meaty arm the second she walked in. He walked Natasha to the bar.

Miguel ordered two beers. "Two Budweisers."

"I don't drink beer."

"Then what can I get you?"

"Root beer."

"Root what?"

"Root beer."

"Beer?"

"No, root beer."

"What is that?"

"It's soda."

"Oh. Okay. Is it beer?"

Miguel hardly spoke any English. Apparently, he had no idea what root beer was, but eventually he got one for Natasha. He told Natasha that he was on his way to Eugene, Oregon, where he was promised a plumbing job with his cousin. He told her that he wanted to become a singer one day. He said he had to make some money in order to buy a fancy outfit, then a guitar or an accordion, or something so that he could take lessons and then make a record. As he looked Natasha over, he wasn't sure he was thinking correctly. While standing by the door earlier, he had been looking at other men and the women they were with. He wanted to experience what they were experiencing. He had decided he would get himself a woman no matter what. He had decided he would have the next woman that walked through the door, regardless. And he would. And he did. Just prior to entering *Jefe*'s, panting as she was because of the short walk, Natasha decided that she would have the first man that approached her regardless of who he was. And she would. And she did.

Miguel was very flattering, which was a far cry, since Natasha was mostly used to insults. The nicest thing anybody ever told her was silence. But, Miguel was smooth. He knew the game. He told Natasha everything she wanted to hear. He mentioned things about the beauty that all women possess, though not any one woman in particular. And, mentioned that she had so much more to offer than those other women, which can be interpreted in any number of ways. He mentioned that he had been waiting for a woman like her to walk into the place, which was true, for the most part. He said he might write a song about a girl like her one day. He saw that Natasha was responding positively to these roundabout compliments. He decided, then, to start showering her with compliments, most of which he didn't believe, but that didn't matter. Natasha didn't know the game, so she took everything Miguel was saying seriously. She took it so serious that she invited Miguel back to her apartment after last call. She didn't tell Miguel that she was a virgin. Miguel didn't care one way or another. All Miguel was considering was how in the world he was going to fuck such a huge mass of a woman.

By the time they made it back to Natasha's apartment, Natasha was sweating. There was a certain stink that surrounded Natasha. Natasha smelled it. She didn't care. She wanted to get laid. Miguel smelled it. He didn't care, either. He wanted to get laid, and was growing more and more curious the more he thought about it.

Miguel kissed Natasha the minute they walked into her apartment. Right then, for the first time in his life, he got a taste of root beer, only he didn't know it. He just thought that Natasha had strange, mediciney breath. Soon, Miguel had his hands all over Natasha's breasts. They were huge. He liked that. He also noticed that Natasha wasn't wearing underwear. He liked that, too. If he wasn't certain about his prospects before, Natasha's lack of panties was the clarifying signal. It was on. A few times, as his hands wandered a little lower along Natasha's body, Miguel thought he was still massaging Natasha's breasts, but in fact he was massaging Natasha's rolls of fat. Miguel didn't care one way or another. He was getting some. So was Natasha.

Miguel undressed. Natasha collapsed onto her bed, the way she did when she was watching television, only she wasn't staring at Oprah Winfrey, she was staring at Miguel: the first man who had ever kissed her, the first man to ever stand completely nude before her, the first and only man that would ever have her. Natasha imagined a love session filled with kissing and caressing, like in movies. She even had a preposterous flash where she imagined Miguel lifting her up out of bed, Natasha straddling Miguel's waist, Miguel pushing Natasha against a wall, and fucking Natasha while standing. The engineering alone would have been mind-boggling. Miguel was just thinking he was going to bang the shit out of her. Natasha lifted her muumuu over her breasts. The first thing Miguel noticed were the waves of flesh that made-up Natasha's body. Then he noticed Natasha's pubic hair. And, there was a whole lot of it. He noticed that her pubic hair covered her pubic area and extended beyond her waist, up and over her bellybutton, which he assumed was somewhere within the folds, and the hair nearly wrapped around her waist like a bikini-bottom. At that point, not even that mattered. Miguel had to yank at his member a few times to warm himself up. Perhaps it was the booze, but probably not. He yanked several more times. Miguel climbed aboard. He displaced some flesh with one hand, and maneuvered his penis with the other. Several minutes later, Miguel finished. Natasha hardly felt a thing, what with her masturbating all the time, sticking her fingers and fist up to her wrist in there. Miguel felt many things. He felt dirty. He felt confused. He felt sober. Mostly, Miguel felt like vomiting. He did, the minute he left Natasha on the bed and went outside, his semen dripping out of her vagina, rolling down to her ass, and onto the bed. Miguel never returned.

Natasha didn't purposefully choose that night to get pregnant, it just happened. She didn't mind it, though. She also didn't mind the fact that she never saw Miguel again. At first, she did mind. She went looking for him. For the first couple of months, she went to *Jefe*'s once a month on the same day of the week that she met Miguel. She even wore the same outfit, which she called her "lucky outfit" as she was putting it on. She didn't say this to anybody but herself. She would just enter *Jefe*'s then turn around and go back out if Miguel didn't grab her arm just as she walked in, like he did that first and only night. He never would again. Oh, well.

She didn't mind it when she found out she was pregnant

with twins. The funny thing was that Natasha didn't gain weight while pregnant with her twins. Her weight remained steady, as did her appearance. In fact, she didn't gain weight until after giving birth.

To stick with her Mexican and Russian roots, she named her twin boys Moctezuma and Vladimir. The government of the United States of America supported Natasha and her family. They had all the food they needed. They had their rent and utilities paid for. They had clothes. Natasha even had the luxury of allowing herself packages and packages of blank cassette tapes, which were surprisingly easy to find in Eureka, California, which she used to record radio shows.

Her two boys, once they were old enough, did the grocery shopping. They went to school. They were both very fat. At school they were known as the "double zeros," "fat and fatter," "the sun and the moon." "Here come the sun and the moon," their fellow students would say, respectively, but not respectfully. Moctezuma and Vladimir didn't care. They would tell their mother but she wouldn't care, either. She was always busy with her radio programs. She would send her sons to the electronics store to buy her tapes. They didn't mind doing it, which was good because Natasha had grown so fat that she could no longer get out of bed. All she did at home was eat, record radio shows, and watch television. She never missed the Oprah Winfrey Show. Natasha loved Oprah. Natasha was so proud of Oprah for having lost so much weight. She would clap and laugh and hoot as she watched the show. Her sons didn't mind all the noise their mother would make. The twins also didn't mind sponging Natasha down every week or so. They were one big, happy family.

When Natasha wasn't watching Oprah, she would record every Spanish radio program that she could. She had an old tape recorder that she brought from home. Her father bought it at Sears so that he could listen, while working, to the radio and bootleg tapes that he bought at the swap meet. Steven would use it every once and a while to record his own voice, especially around the third grade. He would conduct interviews with himself, asking himself questions about school and friends and girls that he liked. His answers would always include references to people that either didn't know him, or, if they knew him, didn't want anything to do with him. He would ask himself, in a deep voice, things like, "So, Steven, do you have a girlfriend?"

Steven would answer, "Yes, I do."

"What's her name?"

"Josette Ramírez."

"What grade is she in?"

"She's in third grade, just like me."

"Is there anything you would like to say to her?"

"Yes. I would like to tell her that I love her. I'd like to sing a song to her." Steven would then break into his favorite Hall and Oates song:

> Because your kiss,
> Your kiss,
> Is on my list,
> Because your kiss,
> Your kiss,
> I can't resist,
> Because your kiss is on my list
> When I turn out the lights.

It was silly, but Steven felt good about letting things out. Those people that did know him, that he referenced, did not think about Steven in the way that he claimed in those mock interviews. They all just thought he was retarded. Steven didn't really know that, yet. He didn't care, anyway. He liked recording his voice. He liked the fact that it sounded so strange when it came from the tape recorder's speaker. It only sounded strange to Steven because when he heard his own voice, the vibrations that his voice produced in his body accentuated his voice within himself. Those vibrations didn't occur when he heard the recordings of his voice. Had anybody else heard the recordings, they would have heard Steven's voice the way they had always heard it. Steven stopped recording his voice after his horse riding accident. Two years after the accident, Steven's father stopped listening to music on the recorder because he stopped working, because he stopped living. Natasha kept the tape recorder for herself. She took it with her to college so that she could listen to music while she studied. It obviously wasn't put to use in the way she had intended. But she did use it. Everyday. She would record her Spanish radio programs religiously, sometimes for hours a day. She would carefully listen to the music, and more so to the disc jockeys that would announce the song titles and artists after playing their music. She hoped to one day hear Miguel's name announced, and possibly a title that would suggest a memory of their encounter. Not so that she could hunt him down, and try to reignite their one night of passion; nor did she want to collect from him years of unpaid child support for children he never even knew existed. Natasha just wanted to have a copy of his music that she could share with her children, something for them to be proud of. She has thousands of tapes inside hundreds of boxes that she has saved. It's her collection. She thinks she's going to leave her tape collection to her children after she dies, which she expects will be soon because of her weight. It will be soon. She has her children and her hopes to keep her alive. She hasn't heard Miguel's name, yet.

Is it any wonder that Steven doesn't know about any of this? All Steven knows about Natasha is that she is fat and that she went away to college. He doesn't know about her children, Miguel, or anything else. It's not that he doesn't care. He hasn't thought about her for years. Out of sight, out of mind.

Chapter X

On his way to Seven-Eleven, Steven waved to his neighbor, Louie. Louie, however, didn't wave back. Not because Louie didn't like Steven because he was retarded. Louie didn't mind Steven, although he did think Steven was retarded. The reason Louie didn't waive back at Steven is because Louie only has one arm. The reason Louie didn't use his one arm to wave is because Louie was watering his lawn. The reason Louie was watering his lawn is because Louie doesn't work, because he only has one arm. Aside from missing an arm, Louie is missing both of his legs, which is why he's confined to an electric wheelchair. He lost his legs to diabetes. He was overweight and drank a lot. Many thought that contributed to his diabetes. It didn't help, but his diabetes was inherited from his mother who was long dead, but had died of pancreatic cancer, not diabetes. Still, Louie was born with the predisposition. Aside from his legs, Louie also lost all of his fingers on his remaining arm. That is why, when Louie is watering, he holds the water hose between his bicep and forearm, like a football.

In fact, when Louie was in high school, he was a tremendous football player. He was the only freshman receiver chosen to play on the varsity team. Because of that, Louie was very well respected by his fellow teammates. The cheerleaders liked him a lot, as well. One senior cheerleader in particular, Roselia, liked him so much, that she gave Louie his first hand-job. Louie didn't know it was coming. He was so excited that

Roselia was kissing him, that he never considered moving further with her. Roselia knew she was going to give Louie a hand-job before she even began kissing him. That hand-job was to start Louie's legendary high school escapades, which included screwing quite a few other cheerleaders, a few of the girls who would run with the party crews, and even a few of the quiet, nerdy chicks, who, although Louie wasn't very attracted to them, he screwed anyway because he figured they really wanted to screw him and he was there to please. That hand-job also gave Louie the confidence to play football like a man, because he felt, especially after the hand-job, like a man.

Louie played football like a man. He would take hits, outrun his opponents, and score touchdown after touchdown. Louie's high school football team was league champs every year that Louie played with them. When Louie was a junior, his football team made it to the state championship. Louie was excited because his team had never made it so far.

The game had the typical fervor of a championship high school football game. The fans were cheering. It was a high scoring game. Louie had caught four touchdown passes. Louie's coach had already decided that if his team was to win the game, Louie would be the Most Valuable Player, even though he was only a junior, and there were plenty of seniors who were having the games of their lives. As it turns out, down by four points in the fourth quarter, Louie's team had one last set of downs to win the game. The coach and quarterback all agreed that the ball had to go to Louie. Louie agreed, as well. He had already caught four touchdown passes, and countless others in the regular season.

First down: Louie runs a seven-yard post, and is open in

the end-zone. The ball had left the quarterback's hand before Louie even turned around. Once he did, Louie let the ball fall into his hands. Unfortunately, he also let the ball fall right out. Louie didn't know what had happened. It had never happened before. Sure, he had dropped a few passes before, but never when he was wide open, in the end-zone, with a game on the line. He even kept looking at his empty hands, wondering if, by magical illusion, the ball had just disappeared. The groans coming from the bleachers convinced him otherwise. Louie accepted the error and asked for the ball. He swore it wouldn't happen again.

Second down: Louie runs the same seven-yard post, and is miraculously open again in the end zone. It was the perfect play to call, because the defense would never expect them to run the same play. This time, the quarterback waited until Louie turned around, so as to not catch Louie by surprise, and then threw a bullet—aiming directly at the numbers on Louie's jersey. The ball hit the numbers, then the floor. Louie accepted the error, again, and asked for the ball, again. He swore it couldn't happen again. And, if history has any bearing on the real world, it couldn't happen again.

It could. It did.

Not on third down. The third down play was a hand-off, with hopes that it would catch the defense off guard. It didn't. The team lost three yards. By the fourth down, the team knew they had no choice but to go for it. Louie was given his last chance to prove himself. The quarterback, Chaidez, told Louie in the huddle, "I'm throwing you the ball. Goddamn it, if you drop it this time, I'm going to beat the shit out of you. This is may last chance at this. On two. Ready . . . Break."

It was Chaidez' last chance. Chaidez was a senior. Louie didn't care one way or another. He knew that if the ball came to him, he was going to catch it. It was a done deal.

The ball came to him. He didn't catch it.

The opposing team took over on downs, took a knee, and the game was over. Just like that.

Chaidez didn't beat the shit out of Louie. He did say, after the game, on the way to the locker room, "You're fucking retarded," and nothing else. Chaidez did beat the shit out of himself. He drank the shit out of himself, anyway. At the after party which was thrown at a cheerleader's house—who, before that night was seriously thinking about fucking Louie, but right after the game decided that she would not—Chaidez was so upset that he drank enough tequila to wake-up the next day on the bathroom floor, the toilet next to him filled with his vomit, and his pants soppy with shit. Louie would not be the Most Valuable Player of the game. Not that year, anyway. The following year, Louie's team went all the way: state champions. Many accused Louie of dropping the ball on purpose his junior year, so that he didn't spoil the excitement and sense of accomplishment that came with winning the championship his senior year. Louie didn't do it on purpose. He simply made three mistakes.

Louie didn't go on to play college ball, like most people assumed he would. Instead, he impregnated a cheerleader who, much like Roselia, liked to give Louie hand-jobs. Louie liked that about her. Curiously enough, her name was Rosario, which made Louie think extra hard every time he said her name, so as to avoid a mispronunciation. Louie didn't just like Rosario's ability to pleasure him with her hand. He also liked the blow-jobs, tit-jobs, and the fact that Rosario liked to fuck Louie reverse cowgirl style. All that fucking, it was no wonder he impregnated her.

Louie had to take a job at a sheet metal warehouse in the nearby city of Downey, California, where he drove a forklift. That was where he was to lose his arm. Louie excelled at forklift driving, like he excelled on the football field. He was so good at his job, his manager let him work overtime, and he never let anybody work overtime. Louie was so good that his manager let him close-up the warehouse after Louie was done for the night, after all the other employees had left, and trusted that Louie wouldn't lie about the number of overtime hours he actually put in. Louie never lied.

One night, Louie was stacking pallets of sheet metal after everybody had left. He was gathering all of the pallets in the warehouse and organizing them in rows. It wasn't absolutely necessary, but it was overtime work, and he was saving-up for Los Angeles Raiders season tickets. The first mistake Louie made was stacking the pallets too high. He was trying to conserve space, and that was the main reason for organizing them in the first place. There was one stack of pallets that appeared to be leaning forward. The second mistake Louie made was getting out of his forklift to inspect his leaning stack of pallets. Louie wanted to make sure he had stacked each one straight. Call it personal quality control. The third mistake Louie made was when he decided to manually push the stack back, in an attempt to straighten it out. Although it was ludicrous to think he could move a stack of pallets piled with sheet metal, the pallets did move. They moved maybe a millimeter back, but that was enough to set the momentum of the already leaning pallets forward and onto Louie. The pallets didn't fall directly on top of Louie. Louie was fast. He proved that on the football field. The pallets did, however, land on Louie's right arm. Louie was lucky to be alive, but wished he was dead because the pain he was going through was horrendous. Louie was trapped. He couldn't get his arm out from under the pallets. After two hours, his mind was going through disassociation. His body no longer associated feelings of pain with the pallets on his arm. For a second, Louie thought he would look for something to cut off his own arm. While there were many things in the warehouse he could use, none were at arms length. He thought he would try to gnaw his arm off, the way he had heard coyotes would gnaw their legs off when they got them caught in bear traps. He quickly decided that he shouldn't do that because then he wouldn't be able to drive a forklift with only one arm. He would try to relax, ignore the pain, for the sake of his arm.

  Louie was discovered in the morning by his manager. His manager called an ambulance. The manager jumped into the forklift and lifted the pallets off of Louie's arm as they waited for the ambulance to come. Louie was conscious. He explained to his manger what had happened. He explained that he couldn't feel his arm. His manager said, "Just be glad you're alive." What his manager was thinking was, "God, you're fucking retarded."

  As a result of the accident, and the amount of time his arm spent being crushed by the sheet metal, Louie would lose the arm. He would never return to work. His manager told him he could no longer perform his job, so he wasn't needed anymore. On paper, Louie's boss based the termination on gross negligence, so as to avoid a law suit. There would be no law suit. He also told Louie that he had included in his check eight hours of overtime: the two that he spent working, and the six he spent with his arm under a pallet. What a thoughtful guy. The government of the United States of America was also thoughtful enough to provide Louie with disability. And how.

Once diabetic, Louie would then lose his fingers, then his legs, and is currently losing his sight, in one eye only. Louie still feels phantom pain, twelve years after his pallet injury. He still feels his arm getting smashed by pallets. He still feels his fingers and tries to move them, the way he tried when they were under the pallet. His wife sees him suffering. His wife, Rosario, feels pity for her husband, but only to the extent that the entire neighborhood feels pity for him. She's no longer intimate with Louie. No more reverse cowgirl, no more blow-jobs, no more hand-jobs, no more tit-jobs. In fact, when Louie first lost his arm, he had to learn to masturbate with his left hand, which was okay the first few times because it felt so foreign. When he lost his fingers, he had to learn how to masturbate by rubbing his penis between his stumpy left hand and his belly. It is a lot of work, and the pay-off feels great, but he hardly does it. He wishes his wife would do it for him, like in high school, but she finds him repulsive. She helps him around the house, when she isn't out running errands, or screwing Rudy Christianson, the son of Nick the drunk.

While Steven knows that Louie is missing an arm, both legs, and his fingers, Steven doesn't know that Louie is also missing his hair. Louie didn't lose his hair in an accident, nor to diabetes. Louie lost his hair, the same way he developed diabetes: his DNA. Steven doesn't know that Louie lost his hair because Louie cleverly disguises his hair-loss with a toupee. Another thing Steven doesn't know is that the toupee that Louie wears is the second one Louie has owned. The first one caught fire a couple of years ago, back when Louie was still smoking cigarettes. Louie didn't give up smoking cigarettes because of the toupee incident, but because it was such an ordeal just to get a cigarette, much more to get it lit, smoke it, then extinguish it, what with his lack of appendages. Louie was rolling around in his electronic chair, through the kitchen, trying, using only his mouth, to get a cigarette out of a pack on the counter. His wife was out with Rudy. Louie didn't know she was with Rudy, but he did know she was out. After several cigarettes ended-up on the floor, one ended-up in his mouth. He rolled over to the stove and pushed the ignition knob with his stumpy hand. When Louie leaned over to light his cigarette, his toupee caught fire. Louie began to panic. He tried to pull off the toupee, but he didn't have fingers. He shook his head violently, until the toupee fell to the ground, and his eyes spun within their sockets. He couldn't stamp out the fire, because he didn't have any legs. Instead, he rolled over the flaming toupee several times. Eventually, the toupee went out, but by then it was useless, and needed to be replaced. Poor guy.

Steven doesn't feel pity for Louie. He likes Louie, and talks to him every chance he gets. Like today. Although Louie didn't wave at Steven, Steven went up to Louie anyway. Steven told him, "Rah-rah. Rah. I'mah ... I'mah. I-I-I. I'mah. Kaymh-Kaymh." What Steven was trying to tell Louie was that he was going to kill his mother and that he was on his way to Kmart to buy a knife.

Louie didn't understand a word. All Louie said was, "Okay." Then, as Steven walked away, Louie said, under his breath, "Yeah, yeah, whatever fucking retard." Then he went back to watering, holding ever so tightly to the hose.

Chapter XI

Right then, Steven heard a familiar jingle. It was the theme to Popeye the Sailor Man. It wasn't the up-tempo song you hear when Popeye eats his spinach. It was the song you hear when the cartoon opens and Popeye is walking with his usual bounce, smoking his pipe, and singing. Only when Steven heard the jingle, it wasn't being sung by Popeye. The jingle was distortedly coming from an ice cream truck. Steven ran to the truck, waving his arm, gesturing it to stop.

Oddly enough, the driver of the ice cream truck is afflicted with something similar to the affliction that must have caused Popeye to have such a moniker. The ice cream truck driver, Agustin—or Dead-eye, as he's known around the neighborhood—has a dead eye. The eye never actually died, because it was never really alive. He was born with it. It's still in his head. It just uselessly floats in his socket, staring up at the inside of his brow. The pupil is barely visible. People have always made fun of Dead-eye. They'd call him "Dead-eye," "that dude with the fucked-up eye," "the guy whose eye is all retarded," "*ojo chueco*." Dead-eye never really cared. He knew his eye was strange. He came to grips with it a long time ago. His girlfriend, Griselda, also came to grips with it. She didn't care that his eye was dead. She liked Dead-eye for what he was: an ice cream man. Because he was an ice cream man, he had a little bit of money. That was all the money Griselda needed to get her fix.

Griselda is the neighborhood crack whore. There were

more women in the neighborhood that did crack, but Griselda was the only one that wore it like a badge. She is blonde, with brunette threatening to pour out of her head. She is skinny to the point of emaciation, knobby on the knees, jaw, and elbows. Her teeth look like she exists on a diet of rocks and broken windshield glass. Griselda wasn't a whore, but the people in the neighborhood still referred to her as "the crack whore," "wasted bitch," "the filthy skank that hangs out with Dead-eye." She did crack. She knew it, and didn't care who else knew. Dead-eye knew it. He didn't care. She also did crystal-meth, which she bought at Tony's Hof Brau from the neighborhood crystal meth dealer, Fat Dan, who isn't fat.

Dead-eye doesn't do hard drugs. He drinks a lot of beer and smokes marijuana. Anybody that has ever bought an ice cream off of Dead-eye knows that Dead-eye likes to drink beer. He reeks of it. When he hands you a 50/50 bar, Fudgecicle, or Big Stick, you can't help but get a tremendous whiff of Lazer Malt Liquor. It's his drink of choice. It has never gotten him into trouble. It doesn't affect his driving. He's always very conscientious. The worst thing that has ever happened while being drunk and selling ice cream was his giving of incorrect change. For some reason, it is always in the favor of the customer, so Dead-eye isn't even aware that he has ever made an error. He once sold a seventy-five cent snow-cone to a little girl who gave him a dollar. He gave the little girl four quarters as change. She didn't say anything. Neither did he, except, "Thank you." Dead-eye doesn't catch his errors because he doesn't have a regimented way of keeping track of his sales or inventory. When he runs low on a particular ice cream, he goes and buys a box at Art's Liquor, whose owner,

Pedro Chafas, also doesn't take inventory. As long as Dead-eye makes a little profit, that's all that matters to him, and to Griselda, the crack whore.

Steven never took any extra change from Dead-eye. Steven hardly ever bought anything. The only thing Steven ever bought from Dead-eye was Freeze Pops. Steven loved them. He especially liked the green ones, although they didn't taste like anything green. One would think they would taste like apple, or mint, or lime, or something like that, but they don't. They taste like sweet ice. Steven still loves them. He also loves the fact that they only cost a quarter. Since Steven is always on a strict budget, that's pretty much all he can afford. Today, however, Steven decided to splurge.

When he finally caught-up to Dead-eye's ice cream truck, Steven didn't hear Dead-eye mumble to himself, "Oh, great. Here comes that fucking retard." Steven did hear Dead-eye say, "Hey, what can I get you?"

Steven pointed at a picture of a Freeze Pop, the green one, on the outside of the truck. "Reen. Ree-ree-reen. Foh-foh-foh," Steven said, pointing with one hand, holding-up three fingers on the other. What Steven was trying to say was that he wanted four green Freeze Pops.

"You want a Freeze Pop?"

"Yeah. Yeh-Yeah. Foh-foh-foh," he said, again, holding up three fingers.

"You want three?"

"Y-yeah. Y-yeah."

Dead-eye turned around, shuffled a bit, then turned back. "Here you go." He handed Steven three Freeze Pops. "Seventy-five cents."

"Wah-wah-wah," Steven said, holding up one finger.

"Another one?"

"Y-y-yeah."

Dead-eye turned around again, while saying to himself, "Then why didn't you tell me you wanted four in the first place, you fucking retard?" Dead-eye shuffled a bit again, then turned back again with another green Freeze Pop.

"That's a dollar."

Steven gave Dead-eye the dollar. As Steven was trying to bite open his Freeze Pop, a bit of plastic that he spit out of his mouth landed near the foot of an approaching customer. Steven turned slightly and saw that it was Mrs. Montes and her daughter, Elizabeth. Steven is afraid of Mrs. Montes. The reason Steven is afraid of Mrs. Montes is because Mrs. Montes hates Steven.

There are three reasons why Mrs. Montes hates Steven:

The first reason Mrs. Montes hates Steven is because Steven is retarded.

The second reason Mrs. Montes hates Steven is because she suspects that Steven has been stealing her underwear. He has. She has never seen him do it, but she has caught him sneaking into her backyard. She once saw him walking up her driveway, past her kitchen window. She was doing dishes. Steven was on his way to see if Mrs. Montes had any of her panties drying on the clothesline. He didn't particularly like the style of panties that Mrs. Montes wore. They were regular cotton brief panties. All Steven knew was that she left them to dry on her clothesline. Steven was just making his usual rounds.

When Mrs. Montes saw Steven walking into her yard,

she gave a sort of hiss; a loud hiss like one would give a cat or dog if they were somewhere they were not supposed to be.

"Shhht!"

Steven didn't bother to see where the noise was coming from. He knew it was addressed at him. He knew he was someplace he was not supposed to be. He just did an immediate one-eighty and walked out of Mrs. Montes' driveway. Mrs. Montes wasn't going to let him off that easy. She ran to her porch and yelled after Steven. "I know what you were going to do. You better stay out of my yard! Next time I see you, I'm going to call the police! Stay out of people's yards, fucking moron!" All of this was said in Spanish. Steven understood.

The person that didn't understand was Steven's mother. When Mrs. Montes went to tell Steven's mother, she banged on the front door and waited the couple of minutes it took Steven's mother to open the door, tying on her robe. She knew somebody was home. She could hear the theme from Cops coming from inside the house. Mrs. Montes told Steven's mother what she suspected. All Steven's mother could say, standing at the threshold of her home in a robe, was, "I don't understand. Steven would never do anything like that. I know that Steven isn't normal, but he would never do anything like that. I really don't understand." She didn't understand. She shut the door, disrobed, and prayed to Jesus Christ that it wasn't true. "Please, Jesus Christ, my Savior. Please don't let this be true, Heavenly Father." That was all it took, as far as Steven's mother was concerned.

The third reason Mrs. Montes hates Steven is because of what Steven did to her daughter, Elizabeth. It wasn't anything bad, as far as Steven was concerned. Then again, he is a retard. But really, it wasn't. Steven was walking, as he always did, by Mrs. Montes' house. He saw Elizabeth playing with a jar of bubble solution, dipping the wand, and spinning in order to create bubbles. She was successful on her own, but it occurred to Steven that she would be more successful if he picked her up and swung her around. It was a sincere thought. Steven's father used to do it to Steven when he was a boy and he was blowing bubbles. Steven's father would lift him in his hard, plumber hands, and swing Steven around in a circle until all Steven could see was a wash of colors and a flurry of bubbles popping out of the little, blue wand he held in his tiny hand. He giggled to tears. His father would then put Steven on the floor and Steven would stumble around until the fluid in his ears stopped sloshing around. Steven was too big for that now, and his father was dead. But Steven figured that it would be a treat for the little girl. It was. Steven picked-up Elizabeth and spun her around until she was giggling like he had as a child. Steven put her down and she stumbled around, and laughed hard—so hard that her mother heard her and came out running. She saw Steven standing near her daughter, so she chased him down the block as though he was Frankenstein's monster. She was yelling as she ran. "You stay away from my daughter you fucking retard. If I ever see you lay a finger on her again, I'll kill you." All, of course, in Spanish. Steven understood, although he didn't understand what the big deal was. He knew enough not to bother trying to reason with Mrs. Montes, based on the anger in her voice. Had he attempted, his stuttering nonsense would have gotten him another earful from Mrs. Montes. It was best that Steven just quietly walked away. Steven now makes it a point to stay as far away from Mrs. Montes, and her daughter, as possible.

At the moment, by the ice cream truck, it wasn't possible. She was standing right next to him. She was staring at him. Elizabeth was there too, only Elizabeth was smiling. Mrs. Montes wasn't. She held her daughter closer to her waist and told her, while staring at Steven, "Don't look at that crazy idiot." Elizabeth continued to look, despite her mother's direction. Steven just looked at the floor, sucked on his Freeze Pop, put the three others in his pocket, and quietly walked away.

Chapter XII

As soon as Steven finished his first Freeze Pop, he chewed open another one, and then another one, turning the tartar that frames each tooth in his mouth green. By the time he made it the block and a half to Seven-Eleven, he had finished all four.

Standing in front of Seven-Eleven was a familiar sight. It was a panhandler named *Chile*. *Chile*, like Steven, is retarded, by definition. That is to say, *Chile* is also schizophrenic. Unlike Steven, *Chile* was never diagnosed. While *Chile*'s schizophrenia is mild, it would be enough to grant him financial and medical attention from the government of the United States of America. Since *Chile* has never sought attention of any kind, other than the attention from people who are entering and exiting Seven-Eleven, *Chile*'s schizophrenia remains a secret. Unlike Steven, *Chile* has never been called a retard. He's been called lazy, beggar, bum, panhandler, *pinche pediche*. *Chile* doesn't know this. He doesn't even know that people call him *Chile*, because nobody has ever spoken to him, except Steven. People have yelled at him. In fact, when he used to panhandle outside of Art's Liquor, Steven's neighbor, Tony Chafas, chased him away and told him to never come back. Tony said, "Get the fuck out of here you lazy bum." *Chile* did get whatever fuck he had out of there, and found his way to Seven-Eleven. That move proved to be far more lucrative.

Chile hasn't always been a panhandler. *Chile* hasn't always been *Chile*. He was born Jorge. Jorge, or Jorgie as his family would call him, appeared to have as much potential as any kid in his school, but he refused to reach for it. He failed at everything. He wasn't stupid. He was lazy. That's what his teachers always said. They wouldn't call him stupid or lazy. They would say things like, "It's not that Jorge can't do the work, he just refuses to do the work." The translation of stupidity and laziness was given by his parents.

Jorge's parents attributed their child's apparent stupidity to their insistence of following through with a marriage between cousins. Jorge's parents were cousins. Not distant cousins, either. First cousins. His mom and her dad were siblings. Naturally, as children, Jorge's parents spent a good deal of time together, what with frequent family gatherings, and all. They fell in love in their small town as teenagers—there weren't many partners to choose from—and ran off together, leaving Mexico in order to live the American dream, where else, but the United States of America. It was romantic. It was love. While they have more than one child, the little potential that Jorge had was the only potential among any of the sibling. That conclusion was drawn because Jorge is the only male in the family. Jorge's parents figured that their three daughters—who, according to Jorge's parents, may or may not have had a mental incapacity—would marry, and never have to worry about sustenance, as long as they chose their mates wisely. Logic suggested that the girls should be fine in life. While they all married, none of Jorge's sisters chose their mates wisely. Two married gang members doing life in prison for murder, on separate counts, in separate situations. The other married the part-time cashier at the Seven-Eleven in front of which Jorge would eventually stand.

That explains why *Chile*, or Jorge, or Jorgie, has yet to be asked to leave. As long as the customers didn't complain to anybody that actually cared, Jorge could remain in his position as the panhandler of Seven-Eleven. As long as Jorge stayed out of trouble, his parents didn't care what Jorge did with his life. As far as Jorge's parents know, he's out all day looking for a job. Jorge's parents don't care that he doesn't help the family by paying rent. All they know is that their poor, stupid, lazy child has finally gotten off of his ass and is trying to make a better life for himself. He is.

Chile's move to Seven-Eleven is slowly getting him to that better life a handful of change at a time. He gets enough change by standing in front of Seven-Eleven. He makes enough money in a couple of hours to get himself drunk and fed. He even gets free entertainment, on occasion. He was really amused on day when he saw an old veteran high on PCP. The old veteran wasn't a veteran of any war with regards to the United States military. He was a veteran gang member. *Chile* was amused by the fact that the veteran was stumbling around in his underwear, exposing the tattoos all over his chest and back, and half of his buttocks, claiming he was Jesus. "I'm fucking Jesus, homes! Fucking Jesus!" *Chile* had seen the veteran when the veteran wasn't high. When the veteran wasn't high, he wasn't claiming to be Jesus. He wasn't claiming to be anyone special. He wasn't anyone special. He was just looking to get a forty-ounce bottle of Lazer Malt Liquor. Just like anybody else. *Chile* would ask him for spare change. If the veteran was in the mood, he'd dig into his pocket, open a palm full of coins, keep the quarters and dimes for himself, and hand the nickels and pennies to *Chile*. Nothing special.

The veteran was only special to *Chile* on the day that the veteran thought he was Jesus. *Chile* didn't even bother asking the high, half-naked veteran for spare change that day, he was so amused. He even considered giving the veteran some of his change as a "thank you" for the entertainment he gave *Chile*, the way one might throw some change into the shoe box of some street performer along the boardwalk of a beach, or the sidewalk of a metropolitan city. But that idea quickly faded away. *Chile* figured the veteran would be stumbling around anyway, whether or not *Chile* gave the veteran any of his change. Besides, he didn't have any to spare. Still, that form of entertainment, and the seemingly never ending pockets full of spare change, have kept *Chile* in front of Seven-Eleven. He hasn't considered getting a job since he moved from Art's Liquor to Seven-Eleven.

Steven doesn't think *Chile* is retarded. Steven thinks *Chile* is his friend. Steven likes *Chile* because every time Steven goes to Seven-Eleven, *Chile* gives Steven his empty beer bottle. He always has one, and it's always freshly empty. Steven likes those that are freshly empty best because it is easy for Steven to peel off the labels. Every time Steven adds a bottle to his massive collection, he makes sure to peel off the label, which is why Steven only has hundreds of empty bottles in his collection, not thousands. Steven is very meticulous about it, too. He starts by lifting each corner of the label. The corner that lifts easiest will be his point of entry. If the bottle is wet with condensation, Steven pulls at the looser corner, tugging slowly while lifting away the label with another finger. He's done this many times. If the bottle and label are moist enough, the label peels right off. He spends the next few minutes scratching off, with his pinky nail, the residual glue that sticks to the bottle. Then, with his fingers, he rubs off the glue that couldn't be scratched off. Finally, with his white T-shirt, he polishes off whatever smudges are left. The bottle is then ready to be added to his collection.

 If the bottle is dry, the process is far more time consuming. In that case, Steven, again, starts by lifting each corner of the label. The corner that lifts easiest will be his point of entry. Rather than just pull and tug and lift, Steven adds his breath to the process. He breathes on the bottle as he pulls and tugs and lifts. The moisture in his breath condensates, allowing the label to slowly peel away. Steven spends much more time on a dry bottle. There is also a greater chance of the label tearing, which renders the bottle useless. When the label tears, Steven just throws the bottle away. He doesn't like when that happens. He likes the label to peel right off. He's done it hundreds and hundreds of times.

 Steven might actually have had nearly thousands of bottles in his collection had they not disappeared once from their location at the train tracks, against the wall of the paper factory. Steven was devastated when that happened. It was long ago, when he first started collecting bottles. It was a good time for Steven because some soda bottles, back then, came with Styrofoam labels that peeled right off, without any fear of leaving behind residual stickiness. The ease allowed for an immense collection. He loved that collection as much as he loves his current collection. Steven cried when he found that all his bottles were gone. What Steven didn't know was that the bottles were taken by a transient man that often walked the neighborhood, draped in a loose, stained, gray sweater, or blanket, dirty and unshaven, pushing around a Super-A shopping cart. It took the transient three trips to move the hundreds of bottles to the transient's own location, which he would later take to a recycling center and cash them in for beer money. Steven had never seen the transient, so he had no idea who was to blame for the missing bottles. For a while, Steven spent days walking around, thinking about who it could have been. He thought it might have been his mother, because he couldn't really pin it on anybody else, but he couldn't imagine how she could have removed so many bottles. He eventually decided to start all over again. Seven years later, his collection was nearly complete.

Chile was ready to give his empty forty-ounce bottle of Budweiser as soon as he saw Steven limping up to him. *Chile* didn't like to drink Lazer Malt Liquor. He figured he could afford a better brand.

"Hey, Steven. I have a bottle for you. I just emptied it. Look." *Chile* took the bottle out of a brown paper bag and shook it to prove he wasn't lying. He added, "Do you have any change?"

Steven took the bottle. He ignored *Chile*'s question. Instead, he told *Chile*, "Hassah, hassah, hassah. Imuh-I-I-I-Imuh. K-K-Kmuh. Kmart," and walked away with the empty. Steven was trying to thank *Chile* and tell him that he was on his way to Kmart to buy a knife so that he could kill his mother. *Chile* didn't catch any of what Steven said. All *Chile* could say, under his breath, was, "Whatever, fucking retard."

Steven took the bottle to the alley behind Seven-Eleven. He sat on the black, asphalt floor, between two drying pools of urine, leaned against the stucco wall, and began his label-peeling ritual. Above him, written on the wall in black spray paint, was the word "Stoners," followed by the Roman numerals "XIII," subscripted by the word, "Dreamer." The graffiti was written by a gang member named Dreamer, who was in a gang called the Stoners XIII. The gang called themselves the Stoners because of the fact that they were always smoking marijuana, causing them to get stoned. They always followed their name with XIII because they felt it was mandatory.

Dreamer was given the name Dreamer on account of the fact that he always said things that his friends thought were retarded. The name was first given to him one night when he and his fellow Stoners were getting stoned and Dreamer said, "Aye, homes, one of these days, homes, I'm going to go to college, homes. Fucking college, homes." Dreamer called everybody "homes." In this case, he was talking to Smiley. Smiley replied with, "Ah, fucking Dreamer, aye. Stop fucking around with that stupid shit."

"Nah, homes. Really, homes. I want to go to college, homes. I want to do something with my life, you know, homes? I don't want to end-up working at Kmart, or some shit like that, homes."

"C'mon, Dreamer. Don't fuck around, aye."

The name Dreamer stuck. Until then, Dreamer was known as Mouse, so one could say it was a step up. Dreamer continued his thoughts on college, but never spoke of them again. In fact, he thought he might go on to study gang culture, if there was such a major, and write about the sensationalist correlation between the desire to write graffiti and the desire one has to see their name on the marquee of a theater.

Dreamer could never put his idea to words. He knew it was there, embedded somewhere in the part of his brain that he has yet to put to good use, but in the meantime, he would continue with his own graffiti. Research.

Steven didn't know Dreamer. He was focusing on the bottle. The label was coming off nicely. A few minutes into the removal, he was almost halfway through. He didn't notice the graffiti. Another thing Steven didn't notice was a red beach cruiser that was racing through the alley, right toward him. It was David, Fat Dan's marijuana selling brother who, unlike Fat Dan, who is skinny, is fat. David wasn't looking for Steven. He was just on his way to make a delivery. Steven didn't know. All Steven heard was the muffled hum of the beach cruiser's tire treads rolling on the alley's asphalt. That sound made Steven look up to see the beach cruiser swerve as it came very close to him. It's not like David hadn't seen Steven there. David just liked to mess with people. This time, it was Steven with whom he was going to mess. He had no intention of hitting him with the beach cruiser. Just scare him a bit. David did scare Steven just a bit, but, more so, David distracted Steven. David distracted Steven from his bottle for only a second. That was all it took because when Steven looked at the bottle in his hands, he saw that the label had torn. Steven was upset, but not too much. He would have liked to have the big, brown, forty-ounce bottle of Budweiser, but he would much have preferred a green bottle. He needed green bottles to even out his collection. So, Steven stood up, placed the empty bottle of Budweiser with the torn label on the floor, and continued his walk to Kmart.

Chapter XIII

It takes Steven a long time to get from point A to point B. It doesn't matter to Steven that it takes him so long. He really doesn't have much else to do during the day. The reason it takes Steven so long to get anywhere is because Steven has a severe limp. It isn't the type of limp one has after spraining an ankle, either. Nor is his limp like "the shuffle" one might associate with those that take the medication prescribed to Steven. He doesn't take his medication, after all. It is the type of limp similar to the type of limp an old man who has suffered a stroke might have. His right leg moves as gracefully as anybody else's. It's his left leg that he drags along side of him. Steven never had a stroke. He just had a really bad case of athlete's foot.

It was bound to happen what with Steven's walking everywhere, worn-out shoes, filthy bathroom, and failure to change his socks. All of those things factored into it. It started as mild as any case of athlete's foot. Steven noticed it because his feet stunk a bit and his feet itched. He didn't mind the stink too much. It was hardly noticeable, unless he rubbed between his toes, or scratched beneath his toenails. It was the itching that was getting to him. He would sometimes walk barefoot on the concrete, rubbing the soles of his feet as he walked, the way someone purposefully rubs the soles of their shoes on the carpet in order to collect static so that they could shock somebody. Steven would rub his feet on the concrete in an attempt to stop the itch. Once the itch was satiated, his feet felt like they were on fire. They weren't, but they were raw and threatening to bleed. The stink continually increased—spreading from his toes, to the balls of his feet and his heels—as did the itch. When Steven would take off his worn out shoes with the flapping soles, he would be taken aback by the smell of Parmesan cheese and garbage water. His old socks, nearly clear as women's stockings, would be yellow and a bit crispy at the toes and heels. He would peal his socks off, fabric sticking to his soles of his raw feet. You would swear that when he put his socks on the floor, they could stand on their own. He would then scratch his feet, peeling what looked like blisters off from in between his toes. He would then smell his fingers, scratch, smell his fingers, and scratch. The itch became so intense that, one night, while in bed, the itch didn't let Steven sleep. So he started scratching his feet. He would scratch with his toe nails, one foot scratching the other, but soon would have to really dig in there with his hands if he wanted better results. He scratched and scratched until the itch went away. In the morning, Steven noticed that his fingers had dried blood on them. He didn't know it was blood. He thought it might be shit, but he wasn't sure, so he smelled them. They didn't smell like shit or blood. They smelled like his gnarly feet. He didn't know what had happened until he stepped off of the bed. That was when he felt the pain. It nearly made him collapse. He saw that on the bed were shavings of his skin—powdery, white residue and thick, curling strips that were yellowing.

It was the pain that had Steven's attention. It was magnified when he stepped into the shower, what with the hot water. This made an already short, never thorough shower even shorter and less thorough. He never dried his feet, which didn't help. He had a hard time pulling on the socks that he had pealed-off the night before, the pain of the ravaged feet plus the friction created by the moisture of the shower water, especially around his ankles. He limped for days, until infection kicked in and, naturally, he got a fever. He tried to tell his mother that his feet were hurting him, his left one, in particular. He told her, while hopping on his right leg, "Muh-fuh. Muh-muh-muh-fuh. Muh feet."

"Well then, go to the bathroom." Steven's mother, obviously, misunderstood. She did, however, understand that something was wrong when Steven lifted his pant leg and showed his mother his knee, which had swollen to the size of a football.

"Good Lord! What happened, Steven? Did you fall? Jesus Christ, Heavenly Father, can you please help my son?" Steven didn't bother answering. Neither did Jesus.

After a doctor had initially looked at Steven's knee and ordered an X-ray, the doctor had concluded that the swelling of the knee must be the result of a spider bite, because the flesh around the knee hadn't revealed any trauma. In order to get a better look, the doctor asked Steven to disrobe. It wasn't until Steven started to disrobe for the doctor, and took off his shoes that the doctor changed his diagnosis. The smell, while staggering, was leading the doctor toward Steven's feet. When the doctor put on his surgical mask and pulled off Steven's sock, he saw the problem. Steven's toes were fat with pus, turning gray. The doctor said that Steven had a terrible infection that must have spread to the knee, and that he might have to perform an amputation. That doctor was always quick to draw conclusions. So was Steven's mother, so she said the only thing that she could say in a critical moment such as this: "Oh, Jesus Christ, help us."

It was actually the doctor that helped them. Steven's knee was operated on. It was cut open and the accumulated infection that made his knee swell-up to the size of a football had to be scraped away, he was given many prescriptions for antibiotics, and would need months of physical therapy to get his left leg back to normal. Steven's knee eventually went back to normal. That is, it went back to normal size. It no longer resembled a football. The scars left by the stitches, however, did have a striking resemblance to the large stitching on a football. The prescriptions were never filled. Instead, Steven's mother went to Art's Liquor, which doubles as a back-room pharmacy stocked with prescription drugs imported from Mexico, and got a box of penicillin. She also prayed a good deal for a speedy recovery. While he did recover, mostly thanks to the penicillin, his lack of physical therapy left him limping. "The Lord, Jesus Christ, will take care of you, Steven."

Steven has gotten used to the limping. Steven still walks everywhere, only now it takes him longer than before. His shoes still wear-out fast, and his feet still stink, but a serious infection has yet to return.

It took Steven an hour and a half to get to the shopping center where Kmart was located. He was hungry, though, so he went to the nearby Tacos Mexico. He wasn't going to buy any tacos because it wasn't Taco Tuesday, when the tacos are sold at half price. While the tacos are only fifty cents each, Steven only eats them when he can get them for a quarter. When it wasn't Taco Tuesday, instead of getting tacos, Steven would just ask for a cup of water and eat the radishes that are left out to fix the tacos. The guys that worked behind the counter didn't care that Steven ate the radishes. They were busy cooking, talking about their lives in Mexico, and singing along to songs on the radio. When Steven walked in, one of the cooks was singing particularly loud and with much intensity to a song by Ramon Ayala that went:

> *El día que yo me muera,*
> *No voy a llevarme nada.*
> *Hay que darle justo al gusto.*
> *La vida pronto se acaba.*
> *Lo que pasó en este mundo,*
> *No mas el recuerdo queda.*
> *Ya muerto voy a llevarme*
> *No mas un puño de tierra.*

To Steven's surprise, Nick the drunk was sitting at a booth with a taco in his hand and several balls of foil that had, at some point, undoubtedly housed a dozen other tacos.

"Hey, Steven, what brings you way out here?" Steven sat down on the seat across from Nick.

"Rah-lah-loh. Rah-lah-loh. Tac-tac-taco." Steven was trying to tell Nick that he was on his way to Kmart, but decided to stop off for some free radishes, but not any tacos.

"You don't say. But it isn't Taco Tuesday." Nick had interpreted Steven's mumbles as Steven saying that he was hungry and decided to get some tacos.

"Rah. Rah. Muffuh-muffah." Steven was saying that he was going to kill his mother.

"Yeah, the tacos are small, but they're so cheap. I don't

know how they do it. They stay open twenty-four hours a day, seven days a week, selling tacos, and for only fifty cents!" Nick then leaned into Steven, crooking his finger as though telling Steven to get closer. Nick looked to either side and said, "I think this place is run by the Mexican mafia. La M. It must be where they launder their money. It must be. I mean, come on. They have something like five restaurants within a mile of each other, they're always open, and they sell tacos for fifty cents—twenty-five cents on Tuesdays. Come on. It must be run by the mafia." Steven didn't know what Nick was talking about. Nick did, though.

Nick stopped whispering. "The tacos are good, especially with that red salsa. But, goddamn, they make me have to shit." Nick always talked about shitting. Steven liked when Nick talked about shitting. He would say things like, "Goddamn, here comes James Brown," and "I have to send a fax," then come out of the bathroom waving his hand in front of his face and say, "I think there's a dead body in there."

What Nick didn't know was that there was a dead body in there. Two dead bodies, in fact. Not at that moment, but on two separate occasions. One was a gang member that was stabbed in the stomach sixteen times by his fellow gang members that followed him in there one night with that sole intention. They thought he wasn't being loyal enough because he often questioned motives and was always trying to reason things out. He was just inquisitive. Dead, nonetheless. The other person that died in there was a high school jock. He was killed by his psychotic girlfriend who also thought he wasn't being loyal. She only stabbed him once, but he hit his head on the porcelain sink on his way to the floor. His psychotic girlfriend grabbed his hair and banged his head against the tile floor to make certain he would never get up again. He wouldn't. She was psycho, but thorough.

This time, however, Nick said, "I really have to shit. And, you know how it is: when you have to, you have to. Right, Steven?"

Steven thought about that for a second. Nick stuffed the last taco into his mouth, balled up the remaining foil, and stood up. He paused to think for a second as he chewed.

"Like Confucius says, 'Go to sleep with itchy ass, wake-up with smelly fingers.'" Nick laughed as he stood up. "And that goes for everything. You know what I mean, Steven?" Nick didn't wait for a response. He disappeared into the bathroom.

Steven knew what he meant. Somewhere deep down Steven knew what Nick meant, but on the surface, only literally.

Chapter XIV

Steven left Tacos Mexico. He didn't even eat any radishes. He thought about what Nick had told him, but only for a second. He had other things on his mind like his bottles, and the Rambo knife he had to buy at Kmart.

Outside of Kmart, Steven saw a man dressed in a white suit and the hat of a sea captain holding a white coffee can. The man was asking for donations that would go to helping sick and starving Central American children. The coffee can no longer held coffee. It held the coins that people were asked to spare. Steven saw the man and immediately felt sorry for him. He didn't feel sorry for the man's cause, but rather for the pain the man must be enduring to sustain the strength that it takes to carry the coin filled coffee can. Steven could relate because, as a child, Steven's father would force Steven to carry the coffee cans that held the extra change that he would empty out of his pockets every night when he got home from work. Aside from getting the shit beat out of him, Steven would have to do this whenever he got punished. Only Steven didn't have to carry them in front of Kmart. Steven had to carry a coin-filled can in each of his upturned palms, while his arms had to be extended like a bird spreading its wings. To make things more difficult, Steven would have to do this while kneeling. While simply kneeling wouldn't appear to make matters any worse, what would make matters worse would be the dry rice that Steven's father would sprinkle on the ground. The pain in Steven's arms would be equal to the pain the rice would cause as the hard, tiny pieces embedded themselves into Steven's skin, against the bones of his knees. He would endure the pain, and wouldn't dare complain about his aching arms and throbbing knees because he knew that if he did, the beating he would get would be doubled: one for not following through with his punishment, and one for the initial infraction.

One time Steven's father made Steven inflict this torture on himself. It was the day after Steven's father was in a car accident. The accident occurred on a night that Steven's father drank too much. Steven's father was racing home from a bar because he felt as though he was going to vomit, and didn't want to do so in his truck for fear of ruining it with a smell that was sure to linger for years. He knew he was going to vomit because, after drinking steadily for six hours, his head was spinning in one direction, and his eyes were spinning in the other direction. This awkward movement caused his truck to spin in a counterclockwise direction after having misjudged his speed going into a left turn. His truck would eventually stop spinning as soon as it slammed into a parked car. His head and eyes stopped spinning as well. Steven's father soon noticed that the impact was so strong, as was his grip upon impact, that it caused him to bend forward the steering wheel, which was bent so far, it would have almost been touching the windshield, had the windshield still been there. The shattered glass from the windshield peppered the asphalt with blue-green crystals. Steven's father sat in his wrecked truck for a few seconds. He looked himself over and was surprised that nothing had happened to him: no apparent cuts or pain. More so, he was surprised that nobody had stopped to see if he had survived, or if he needed an ambulance. So, he jumped out of his ruined truck and ran home.

When he got home, Steven's father reported his truck stolen. When he got off of the telephone, Steven's mother asked what had happened. He said, "Nothing. Don't worry about it. It's okay, but . . ." Steven's father paused as he sniffed the room, "I think Steven might have shit his pants. It stinks." What Steven's father was smelling was, in fact, shit. Only, Steven hadn't shit his pants. The shit that Steven's father smelled was coming from his own pants. Apparently, the impact with the parked car forced some shit out of Steven's father.

The next day, the police called saying that they had found Steven's father's stolen truck. The insurance called saying they would help fix it. Steven's mother took these calls. Steven's father wasn't able to take the calls because he was in bed, completely immobile. His muscles in his hands, forearms, biceps and triceps, shoulders, neck, chest, back, stomach, ass, thighs, calves, and feet were stiff and sore. Steven didn't know the extent of the soreness that his father was suffering. Steven was just a kid. So, he did what kids are apt to do: he ran up to his father as he lay in bed. Steven just wanted to see how his father was doing. Unfortunately, Steven touched his father, just rested his arms and part of his upper body on him. This sent a streak of severe pain up and down Steven's father's body. The pain was enough to justify a pain for Steven just as severe.

"You idiot," Steven's father said. "You're really going to get it now." With that, Steven got it. He would have to give it to himself this time, but since he had received it many times before, he knew how to do it. Sprinkle some dry rice on the floor, kneel down, a coffee can with coins in each upturned palm of each outstretched arm. Steven cried, but he learned his lesson. His father would justify the abuse to Steven by saying, "You need to learn that when you do something bad, you will get punished. I just don't want you to end-up standing in front of a store, begging people for money." So, the intent was there. And, one can say, the lesson was learned.

Kmart was now called Big Kmart. It hadn't changed in size. It was only the name that was changed. It was still as busy and disorganized as ever. Steven went to Kmart every Tuesday after eating tacos at Tacos Mexico. Every time he went, he looked at the watches that were displayed behind glass. He particularly liked a watch that had Mickey Mouse at the center, his arms spinning and pointing at numbers. Steven loved that watch, and swore that he would one day buy it. He didn't mind the fact that one of Mickey's arms was shorter than the other. Once, after a particularly stoney lunch break, one of Kmart's employees noticed Mickey's arms and told another of his colleagues, "Check it out man. Fucking Mickey's retarded and shit," in an attempt to crack wise. Steven hadn't even realized Mickey's deformity. It didn't matter to Steven, anyway. Steven couldn't even tell time. All Steven knew was that he wanted that watch.

Steven first saw the watch a few years ago when he and his mother went to Kmart. She was going to buy Bob a black hat with big white letters stitched into it that read, "LAPD." It was Bob's birthday. Steven's mother thought it would be nice to buy him a hat that would associate Bob with the Los Angeles Police Department. Steven saw the watch that day.

He stared awhile at it, while his mother walked around the store searching for the hat. Right then, Steven knew he had to have it. He went looking for his mother. When he found her, he grabbed her arm and pulled her to the watch display case. He then pointed at the watch, desperately tapping the glass with his finger, grabbed his wrist, pointed at the watch, and said, "Me-me-me-ree. Me-me-me. Mick-Mick-Mickey." What Steven was trying to say was that he wanted his mother to buy him the watch. Steven's mother translated it exactly that way. Who'd of thought? But rather than buy him the watch, she told him that instead, they would plan a trip to Disneyland and there she would buy him a watch, and maybe even take a picture with Mickey. Maybe Steven could even get on a ride with Mickey, as they had seen in a commercial a few years ago. Steven nearly cried at the thought. He was so happy.

Unfortunately, Steven never went to Disneyland. Steven's mother did, though. In fact, she went the weekend after telling Steven she would possibly take him. She got so excited talking about it with Steven, that she told Bob about the idea, and they went. Steven wasn't invited.

Steven's mother and Bob took pictures with Mickey, got on all the rides, even stayed in the Disneyland Hotel. It was a perfect weekend. Bob was walking around the amusement park sporting his LAPD hat. He was sure that everybody that looked at him feared and respected him for being a police officer. Actually, an LAPD officer that was visiting Disneyland with his wife and daughter saw Bob walking around with his hat on. The officer didn't say it, but he was thinking, "Would you look at this fucking retard?" Bob didn't know what the police officer was thinking. He only knew what he thought people were thinking.

The weekend was made complete by a spontaneous drive to Mexico. It was Steven's mother's idea. She told Bob, "Let's go have lobster in Mexico. Puerto Nuevo. I hear it's cheap. God willing, we could make it there in a couple of hours." They did get there in a couple of hours, but had the scare of their lives when they almost drove off of Highway 1, along the coast of Baja California. Steven's mother was looking at the ocean, and wasn't sure if she saw a boat floating in the water. She asked Bob what he thought it was. Bob looked at it, and slowed down, for whatever reason. Lucky he did because his slowing made the driver of the car behind Bob honk his horn, returning Bob's attention to the curving road ahead of him. Bob slammed on the brakes and turned the wheel in time to have the car screech to a dusty halt along the railing that they would have easily broken through. With their near-death-experience still at the back their minds, Steven's mother and Bob devoured pounds of lobster, drank gallons of Mexican beer, and screwed like newlyweds. They lived it up.

Steven never knew of any of this. He would have been really disappointed. As he looked at the watch, he considered buying it, and getting the knife some other time. He had money, after all. He quickly decided against it because if his mother saw him with the watch, she would never take him to Disneyland, since one of the reasons they were going to go to Disneyland was to get the watch. Steven never considered the fact that a dead mother couldn't take her son anywhere. But that was Steven. He's retarded.

Steven made his way to the back of the store. That was

where Kmart sectioned their Sporting Goods department. As part of their Sporting Goods department, Kmart sold guns and knives. The idea was that the guns and knives would be used for hunting. Some of the guns and knives that were purchased at Kmart were used for hunting. Others were kept for protection. Still, others were bought and used in the fashion that Steven intended.

Steven looked at the knives, which, like the Mickey Mouse watch, were displayed behind a glass counter. There were many different knives: Swiss Army knives, buck knives, hunting knives. However, there wasn't a Rambo knife. Steven wanted a Rambo knife.

The guy in charge of the Sporting Goods department saw Steven looking at the knives. "Aye, homes, need any help?" The guy's name was Ramon, known on the streets as Dreamer. Despite his shaved head, tattoos, baggy pants, and poor language skills, Dreamer got the job based on his physique. He was, after all, going to sell Sporting Goods. Interestingly, Dreamer built his physique while serving five years in prison for stabbing, and nearly killing a rival gang member who was said to have tried to shoot one of Dreamer's friends, Smiley. That said, Dreamer had plenty of knowledge and experience with Sporting Goods.

"Rah-moh. Rah-moh. Rah-moh." Steven was asking for a Rambo knife.

"What, homes?"

Steven pointed at the knives. "Rah-moh. Rah-moh."

"You want a knife, homes? This is a good one. It's solid." Dreamer pulled out a hunting knife with a long, metal blade and black handle. Dreamer admired it for a second, then stabbed the air repeatedly. "This is a cool-ass knife, homes. Take care of business with this shit." He kept stabbing the air.

"Rah-moh. Rah-moh." Steven was still asking for a Rambo knife. Dreamer wasn't listening. He was still admiring the knife.

"This is a nice *filero*, homes. Cheap, too, homes. Be like Rambo, and shit, homie."

Steven's eyes lit up. "Yuh-yuh-yeah."

"You want to take this one, homes? I can ring it up for you right here."

Steven nodded and took out his bag of money.

Dreamer was ringing it up. "$21.65, homie."

Steven handed Dreamer the bag of money.

"Shit, homes. How much you got in there? Want me to count it?" Dreamer counted the money. He took thirty dollar bills aside, and three quarters. Dreamer zipped-up the bag and handed it back to Steven. "Look, homie, so you don't think I'm trying to rip you off, aye." He held up the stack of thirty dollar bills. "Here's twenty-one." He showed the three quarters to Steven. "Here's sixty-five."

"Okay. Oh-oh-okay."

"There you go, homes. Be cool, aye. Your receipt's in the bag, *ese*." Dreamer handed Steven the bag with the knife and receipt in it. Steven put his sandwich bag, with plenty of singles still in it, in his left pocket, and walked toward the exit.

Dreamer would eventually have lunch at Tacos Mexico. He later told his friend Smiley about how he gypped Steven.

"Aye, homes. This fucking retard, homes, he came into the store to buy some shit, homes. He had this big, old bag of cash, homes. He wanted me to count it for him and shit, homes. So I did, homes. But I kept a little for myself, homes."

"Get the fuck out of here. Really? That's cold, foo."

"Yeah, homes. I even showed it to that fucking retard, aye. To his face, and shit! He still didn't know, homes."

"How much you get?"

"I don't know, homes. Like seven bucks, or some shit. So I went and got me some fifty cent tacos, aye. But I think they made me sick, homes."

"That's what you get for ripping off a retard."

"*Serio pedo*, homes. I had to shit right after that, homie. It fucking stunk, too, homes. It smelled like somebody had died in there, aye."

They laughed a little. Before all that, Steven was making his way out of Kmart, none the wiser.

Chapter XV

Had Steven not paid for his merchandise in the Sporting Goods department, and, instead, checked-out at register number fifteen, he would have noticed that his old neighbor, Felicia, was a cashier. Or maybe he wouldn't have noticed. She looked much different. So did Steven. For one thing, they were much older, and hadn't seen each other in more than twenty years. Another thing was that Steven was preoccupied with killing his mother. The funny thing was that Felicia was also thinking about killing her own mother.

Felicia's mother, Guadalupe, had been abusing Felicia since Felicia and Steven were friends. It wasn't so much that Felicia was a bad child. It was that Felicia occasionally made mistakes, as children tend to do, and also the fact that Felicia's father, Snoopy, was in jail. It wasn't Felicia's fault that her father wound up in jail. That didn't matter. Felicia's mother didn't like that she was without a husband. She was lonely. She would take Felicia, as she got older, twice a month to visit Snoopy at the prison. They would talk to each other, only two feet apart, over a telephone, and stare into each other's eyes through glass embedded with chicken-wire. It always made Felicia's mother very upset when Snoopy would tell her that he wasn't going to get out for a very long time and that his stay would be prolonged due to his involvement with other incarcerated gang members who had to establish themselves as strong by beating and killing rival, incarcerated gang members. Felicia's mother would cry as she hung the receiver.

She would allow Felicia to put her hand to the glass. Her father would mirror her actions. Felicia's mother wouldn't press her own hand to the glass. She would just walk away, yanking Felicia behind her. When they would get home, Felicia would take such an extraordinary beating for just about any otherwise trivial mistake, that her mother would be riddled with such an intense guilt that she would apologize and hold her trembling, sobbing daughter in her arms for hours.

While the beatings stopped as Felicia matured, the abuse did not. Felicia's mother would call her a whore whenever she received a phone call from a schoolmate regardless of his or her intentions. She would call her a whore as she pulled Felicia's clothes off and pushed her into a freezing cold shower. She called her a whore as she watched her daughter squirm to avoid contact with the unavoidable spray coming from the shower head, and watched her writhe and curl into a ball as she gave in to the water and the screams. It wasn't so much that Felicia's mother believed that her daughter was a whore. It was just that Felicia's mother was jealous of her daughter's seemingly ease of love, affection, and attention. That was why Felicia's mother would call her a whore, a little bitch, a fucking slut.

Felicia eventually got sick of the abuse, so she ran away and found abuse of a different kind. She ran away from her mother in Steven's old neighborhood to live on her own in a garage, by chance, in Steven's new neighborhood. She swore she would one day kill her mother for all the abuse. She left high school and found a job pushing and pulling carts in the Super-A parking lot. She made it all the way to bagging groceries, when she met Fat Dan. Fat Dan had just ended a relationship with a girl who was missing a left breast because he had shot it clear off of her chest. In fact, the tit-less girl's brother, Juan Silva, worked as a butcher in that very Super-A. Felicia didn't know about any of this. All she knew was that Fat Dan, or Dan as she knew him because he wasn't fat, had some interest in her, some money to spend, and some crystal meth to spare.

Felicia met Fat Dan while watching a Monday Night Football game at a local steak house called Steven's Steak House, on Atlantic Boulevard. Felicia wasn't really watching the game. She was watching the guys who were watching the game: a bubbling sea of shaved heads, some of the heads tattooed, wearing Raider jerseys whether or not the Raiders were playing. The guys that went to Steven's Steak House didn't just go there to watch Monday Night Football games. They went there for the cheap beer and free appetizers. All of the guys that went there thought that the place was an ideal place to watch a football game. They had no idea how a restaurant could possibly make a profit selling pints of Budweiser for two bucks, and serving-up trays loaded with free food. Customers would often ask themselves, "How the fuck does this Steven guy make any money? The beer is fucking cheap as shit and the fucking food is free. He must be retarded, or rich, or something." The owner of Steven's Steak House wasn't retarded. He wasn't rich, per se. In fact, he wasn't even named Steven. He was a guy named Art who actually made quite a bit of money on Monday Nights. The beer cost him forty cents a pint, so he was making a killing off of that. The cheaper the beer, the more beer the customers bought. The more beer the customers bought, the drunker they got. The drunker they got, the more beer they bought. Et cetera. And, the food was not gourmet by any means. Deep-fry a tightly rolled flour tortilla that has been smeared with refried beans and suddenly you have a *taquito*. Cut them in thirds and you've tripled the amount of food that can go around. Given the typical inebriation of the patrons, these were the best *taquitos* in town.

The night that Felicia met Fat Dan, Fat Dan wasn't there for the football game, or for the free food, or for the cheap beer. He was there to sell crystal meth. Felicia didn't know this. All she knew was that Fat Dan looked like a guy who was looking for a girl. He was looking for a girl, or a guy, who wanted to buy some crystal meth. Felicia leaned against the bar, half-watching the game, half-watching Fat Dan. Fat Dan caught a look and went to stand next to Felicia. He knew what that look meant, only this time it meant something other than what he thought it meant. Felicia felt him next to her. She looked at him. Just as Fat Dan looked over at Felicia, just as he was preparing to ask her if she was looking to score some crystal meth, he saw that she was giving him the eyes. Felicia's eyes were telling Fat Dan that she wanted to fuck. Fat Dan knew those eyes. He had seen them before. He was right.

At first, her situation was ideal. She lived on her own, had a decent job that paid for her rent, and a boyfriend that paid for everything else. The fact that Fat Dan beat the shit out of her every once and a while, didn't seem all that bad. Fat Dan would beat the shit out of her whenever he felt the urge to beat the shit out of someone. It could be because somebody owed him money, owed him junk, or owed him a favor. He couldn't just beat the shit out of one of the perpetrators.

They might rat him out to the cops. That situation would be bad for all of those involved. If Fat Dan beat the shit out of a customer, he may lose that customer. If a customer called the cops on Fat Dan, they would lose Fat Dan. These situations just complicated Fat Dan's life. He had Felicia, after all. Whatever it was, Felicia took it. It wasn't that Felicia was a bad girlfriend. She just made some mistakes, like the time she accidentally left a window open in her place after Fat Dan had stored some crystal meth under her bed. That was bad. It wasn't like anybody actually climbed through the window and stole the crystal meth. Fat Dan found the crystal meth just as he left it. It was just that Felicia introduced the possibility of a potential loss for Fat Dan. That was enough. Of course, he beat the shit out of her.

While Fat Dan never shot Felicia's left breast off, he did shoot his sperm into her vagina. He shot her with such ferocity that one sperm cell shot clear into her egg cell that had just made its way out of her fallopian tube. Days later, she knew she was pregnant. She knew she had made a big mistake. She knew that Fat Dan was going to beat the shit out of her when he found out. He did. All Felicia had to say was, "I think I'm pregnant." That was all Fat Dan had to hear. He punched her in the face. As she fell, he punched her on her back, between her shoulder blades, on the top of her head. He kicked her in the ribs and thigh as she curled-up on the floor and cried. He kicked her in the stomach so hard that a little piece of shit popped out of Felicia's ass. It was tiny, but Felicia felt it. Fat Dan didn't know, otherwise he would have beat the shit out of her more for being so disgusting and shitting herself. It wasn't so much that Fat Dan really cared much about whether or not

Felicia was pregnant. It was just that somebody owed him money that was promised to him on that day. Needless to say, he didn't get it.

When Fat Dan saw that Felicia had had enough, he felt guilty for having beaten the shit out of her. He fell to the ground and started caressing Felicia, holding her tightly for minutes before he completely forgot about the news. Apparently, Fat Dan couldn't smell the bit of shit that he beat out of Felicia because he still hadn't asked her to clean herself up. Instead, he remembered how much he enjoyed suckling on Felicia's breasts, which were directly in front of Fat Dan's face. He did suckle and squeezed, and squeezed her arms and her ass as he kissed and suckled her breasts. He undid her pants and started kissing her neck. Felicia didn't move until she felt Fat Dan's skinny fingers slide inside of her vagina. At that point, she got sick of the manhandling and bit Fat Dan's skinny face, right below the eye forcing him to jump to his feet. She left a clean, bloodless gash that should have exposed a cheekbone, but instead revealed a thin layer of yellow fat. Go figure. While Felicia cursed her self-defense as a mistake, she was surprised to see Fat Dan walk out the door of her garage. He drove himself to the *Clínica Médica Familiar* on Olympic and Gerhart, got stitched-up, and never laid another finger on Felicia. In fact, he never even laid eyes on her again, nor on his child, Dan, or Little Danny as he was later known, who was born three months premature at the same Clínica *Médica Familiar* where Fat Dan got his stitches.

Since, Felicia has been working at the Big Kmart as a cashier making just enough money to pay for her garage and to feed herself and her son, Little Danny, who, unlike his father, is fat—short, but fat. She swore that if she ever saw Fat Dan again she would cut his balls off and kill the motherfucker. That was what she told a colleague of hers. She said, "I swear, if I ever see Dan again I'm going to cut his balls off and kill the motherfucker."

"Oh, come on, Felicia. Don't be retarded," said her fat colleague.

Felicia is also fat. That is another reason why Steven would not have recognized her. Steven remembers Felicia as that skinny neighbor with the thick eyebrows who didn't have a penis, but did have a dog named Snoopy that bit him in the face. She remembers Steven as the fat neighbor, with the twin brother who liked to play with dolls, who had his face bit by Snoopy. They just looked different. Felicia has also taken the look of a typical gang affiliated woman: a hood-rat, if you will. Felicia's eyebrows have nearly disappeared. Where it not for two thick, tattooed lines of black ink that look like comets preparing to collide at the bridge of her nose, there would only exist a thin fuzz on her brow. It's not that Felicia plucked her eyebrows almost entirely, rendering them nearly invisible. It's that Felicia has hypothyroidism. The thinning distal eyebrows are a result of that. While her fattiness would also, technically be associated with such a fate, it isn't because she is not yet in her forties. She is in her late twenties, like Steven, although her worn face would force one to guess otherwise. Her weight is due to the fact that Big Kmart has a Little Caesar's Pizza restaurant in it that sells large pizza's for only five dollars. She takes two pizzas home with her every night. She gives one to the wife of the owner of her garage, who watches her son, Little Danny, while she's at work. She splits the other with her son who, while being a fat kid, can only eat two slices. She eats the other six slices herself, after which she stands in front of the mirror looking at her doughy body, lifting her hair, pursing her lips, scooping her breasts, and adds herself to her mental list of killings.

Steven noticed the Little Caesar's Pizza as he was exiting Kmart. He was hungry. He considered buying a pizza with the money he had left in his sandwich bag, but decided against it because he had things to do. While he knew he should be making his way back home, he really wanted that Mickey Mouse watch. He immediately figured that now was as good a time as any to buy it. Just before he exited, just as the man in the white suit and coffee can was preparing to ask Steven for some change to help the sick and starving children in Central America, Steven turned around. He went back to where the Mickey Mouse watch sat beneath the glass and stared at it. He stared at it and watched as both of Mickey's hands moved ever so slightly, but they moved. He called a sales person over who took it out and showed it to Steven.

"Wha-wah. Wha-wha. Wah-watch. Mih-Mih-Mih. Mih-Mih-Mih." Steven was obviously excited.

"You want this watch?"

"Yuh-yuh. Yuh-yuh. Yeah." Steven stuck out his right wrist, hoping the sales person would put it on him.

"Are you sure you don't want to wear it on your left wrist?"

"Luh-luh. Luh. Luh-luh. Leh-leh-left." Steven was trying to tell the sales person that he was left-handed, so the watch should go on his right wrist. Steven still held out his right wrist.

The sales person didn't understand Steven. "Nah. That isn't your left wrist. That's your right wrist."

"Luh-luh. Luh. Luh-luh. Leh-leh-left." Again, pointing at his right wrist.

"That's not your left wrist. That's your left wrist." The sales person frustratingly pointed at Steven's left wrist.

Steven pointed to his right wrist insistently. "Luh-luh. Luh. Luh-luh. Leh-leh-left!"

"Whatever, man." The sales person put the watch on Steven's right wrist. All the while, the sales person was thinking, "Fucking retard."

And, that was really all it took. Once Steven had his Mickey Mouse watch secured around his wrist, he would never take it off again. The sales person even had to shoot the UPC with his UPC reader gun as it dangled from a string from the watchband. Steven had never felt so secure. He had his watch, he knew what he had to do, and he had what he had to do it with. He had his hunting knife in the plastic Kmart bag. That was what he came for, but he left with so much more. He didn't care about his hunger. He had the one thing he has always wanted and the one thing he knew he needed.

Chapter XVI

Steven was on his way home to take care of the business that Mickey Mouse told him he had to take care of. Steven wasn't scared. He wasn't nervous. He wasn't even anxious. He knew what he had to do. He was going to do it, regardless.

He took a different route home. That is, it was different from the route he took when he made his way to Kmart, but the same route he always took home. The route took him down Gerhart, right past Nichola's. Nichola's was a local strip bar. Steven didn't know it was a strip bar. He had never visited it. He always saw it, and noticed that the parking lot was always crowded, but he never imagined that it was filled with horny, drunk men, and desperate, drunk women.

Nichola's was famous for its cheap women and cheap cover charge. By famous, I mean that it was known around the neighborhood for those reasons. Notorious would be more like it. The cover charge was a measly three dollars. Some customers even complained about it. Those that did were allowed a free entrance. So if a potential customer said, "What, aye? Three bucks? Fuck that, homes!" The person collecting the cover charge would say, "Just go inside. Don't worry about it," as a means of avoiding a confrontation. Not very many customers knew about this policy because not very many customers complained about paying a measly three dollar cover charge.

Once inside, patrons would be subjected to Nichola's twelve dollar pitchers of Budweiser. That was the catch. As far as the customers were concerned, twelve dollars for a pitcher was a lot of money, but the benefits of looking at naked women outweighed the price. Not only were the pitchers overpriced, they came in a thirty-two ounce size, which made the idea of paying twelve dollars for them even more absurd. The management made-up for the small pitchers by supplying the patrons with eight ounce glasses, prolonging the pitcher's contents. The patrons were none the wiser. It was the regulars that were wise to the management's shenanigans. They knew that it was a better bargain to buy a three dollar, twelve ounce mug of beer. In the long run, the mug was more cost effective. Then again, most of Nichola's customers are not thinking of cost effectiveness when there are naked women to think about. No basic multiplication or division.

Especially not those customers that are under age. Nichola's is also notorious for their slack enforcement of the law. While they ask every customer for identification, they hardly look at it. They only ask for the sake of asking. While this deters some under-aged customers, those in the know walk right in.

Those in the know are also aware that just about every woman that dances at Nichola's is available for private dances. The extent of the privacy of these private dances has gone as far as the privacy of a customer's home or the motel of their choice. The dancing part of the private dances has been extended to include fucking. It may cost the knowing customer one hundred bucks, but the fantasy that is taking place in the head of every customer in the joint can be fulfilled.

Steven doesn't know about any of this stuff. He isn't in the know about the happenings at Nichola's. He isn't in the know about the happenings of any place. One person that is in the know is José Ciego.

José Ciego is a regular at Nichola's. All the other regulars know him, but none of them like him. José doesn't care because he doesn't know this. He does know that on Tuesday's at Nichola's, one could purchase twenty-two ounce bottles of Budweiser for five bucks a pop. Tuesday's were the only days that José drank beer at Nichola's. But since it wasn't Tuesday, José was just there to see the girls. The girls knew him, too. At least, they thought they knew him. Whenever José went to Nichola's he dressed in a suit and put on some smart-looking spectacles that he once found in the bathroom of a fast-food restaurant. He went to Nichola's thinking that if he looked like a million bucks, the girls would think he had a million bucks. They did, too. Then again, he was the only customer that ever made any effort to dress-up. Most of the other customers were local gang members dressed in their baggy jeans and loose Raider jerseys, or day laborers dressed in dusty pants and sweaty T-shirts. As far as the girls were concerned, José was the man with the money. Little did they know that he didn't even have a job. The reason they didn't know was because José would tell the girls that he was a successful businessman. They all knew he was a successful businessman because José made it a point to tell all the girls that he was a successful businessman. Lucky for José, none of the women ever asked him what sort of business he was in. That didn't matter to the girls. Whatever business José was in, it had to be successful. Just look at the way he was dressed. They all talked about him in the dressing room behind the small stage. Whenever he walked into the place, he was greeted by one of the girls. They took turns talking to him during his entire visit. He would charm the girls. Any one of them would sit on his lap and pour her drink—that was bought for her by another customer—down his throat. José just put his head back and allowed the alcohol to run down his throat as he rubbed the girl's arm and belly, his fingers massaging the Caesarian scar that was hidden underneath her tulle wrap. She would excuse herself by kissing him on his cheek when it was her turn to dance and tell him, "I'll be right back, sweetie. Don't you go anywhere."

"I won't, baby." He really didn't have anywhere to go. And as soon as José said that, another girl was sitting on his lap, pouring her own drink down his throat. If it wasn't one girl, it was another one. By the end of the night, José was as drunk as any of the other customers in Nichola's, without having spent a cent—not even the cover charge.

José has taken home many of the women. Not literally to his own home, but to a local motel. They even pay for the motel. He offers to take them to his house in the hills of Montebello, but they say it's too far and that they have to be back at work within an hour. José doesn't question the girls. He accepts their proposals, fucks them in a dirty motel, and brings them back.

There is one girl who José has not fucked. It is the girl that all the guys at Nichola's want to fuck, but none of the guys have. Her name is Crystal. It is known around Nichola's that Crystal doesn't play that game. People say, "Her? Nah. She doesn't play that game," meaning that she doesn't have sex for money. Still, deep down, she knows that she would if the price was right. José knows that his turn is coming. He just has to talk the other girls into talking him up. He always asks the girls, as they sit on his lap, "So what's Crystal's story?" He asks this with hopes that the girls would pass the message along to Crystal that he is talking about her. They do.

Steven saw José talking to one of the girls in the parking lot as he made his way home. While Steven and José are neighbors, Steven didn't recognize José because he was dressed in a suit. Steven usually saw José dressed in dirty, red sweat pants and a tank-top, sitting on the porch of his parents' house, drinking his father's beer.

José was asking the girl, "So what's Crystal's story?" Before the girl could answer, José saw Steven walking on the other side of the street. He told the girl, "Hey, it's my retarded neighbor." Then he yelled, "Hey, Steven!" José lifted his hand and gave a sort of wave.

Steven didn't hear or see anything. He was just walking. This embarrassed José because he thought that the fact that a retarded guy ignored him was an insult, and this would not impress the girl that he was talking to, much less Crystal, if it ever got back to her. He hoped that she wouldn't share this with the rest of the girls. Just to be sure, he told the girl, "Retarded and deaf. Damn."

José's yell didn't get Steven's attention. He was thinking about his mother, and how he was about to kill her.

José looked, again, at Steven. "Fucking retard," José said to himself when he realized that he wouldn't get Steven's attention. Then he went on talking to the girl, "So, what's her story?"

While José's yell didn't get Steven's attention, a box of Heineken did. It was sitting on the sidewalk beside a parked car.

It was left there by a carload of teenagers that drank the beer just before going into Nichola's. They drank the beer, which they bought at Art's Liquor, before entering Nichola's because they couldn't afford to pay twelve dollars for a pitcher. Steven knew that the box was filled with empty beer bottles because he saw one of the bottles protruding out of the top of the box where it was torn open. The twelve bottles would really help his collection. What Steven didn't know was that there were only ten bottles in the box because the teenagers had stuffed two full bottles of Heineken into their pockets in order to drink them while looking at the naked women of Nichola's. Well, they would look at the naked women for a while first, then go to the bathroom and slam the beer. They'd throw the empty bottle into the trashcan that was usually reserved for soiled toilet paper, but usually ends the night filled with empty beer bottles of brands that the bar doesn't sell. The management is aware of this phenomenon, so they are sure to put a kitchen-sized trash can in the bathroom to accommodate the trash. It beats having to pick up a bunch of empties off of the floor beneath the tables and against the stages.

 Steven limped quickly, as quickly as one can limp, to the box. To Steven's delight, the bottles were freshly emptied. They were still wet with condensation. Steven was excited. At the moment, he forgot about killing his mother. All he could think of was that he had to get to the train tracks as soon as possible. There, he could sit and carefully peel off the labels and add these twelve green bottles to his collection.

 Steven switched his Kmart bag over to his right hand. Steven bent down and grabbed the twelve pack with his left hand, and cradled it like a football because the box's handle was torn when it was opened. The box clinked as he lifted it. Steven liked that sound, but it scared him at the same time. He liked it because the sound meant more bottles. He disliked it because he was afraid that one might break. It was a gentle balance.

Since the sun was still up, Steven could probably get these bottles peeled and set just in time for the sun to strike his collection at just the right angle to reveal the brilliant colored lights that he enjoyed so much.

Chapter XVII

Steven was only four blocks away from the train tracks. He knew he had to hurry because the bottles would soon dry, making the removal of the labels that much more difficult. Besides that, the sun would soon reach that pivotal point that Steven was anticipating.

On his way, Steven passed the *Clínica Médica Familiar*. The *Clínica Médica Familiar* was, as the name implies, a family medical clinic. It catered specifically to the down trodden families that couldn't and didn't have insurance or couldn't afford a private practice. That was why the waiting room at that clinic was always crowded with women surrounded with half a dozen crying children running in between chairs, the sick one of the bunch cradled against her bosom; old, dark-skinned men wrinkled by the sun, coughing chunks into handkerchiefs; gangsters with their pubescent girlfriends sitting nervously awaiting results. Several times, Steven was among them, shaking with fever, his mother sitting quietly, prayers bouncing in her head. He hated that place. It reminded Steven of his mother. But that wasn't why Steven hated that place. He hated it because that was the place where Steven would go to get shots. A lot of people went there for shots. Shots were the quickest way to fight a well established infection, and infections seem to develop well on the neglected. So, it seemed that the clinic was the place to go to for shots, although that wasn't the only service they offered. As far as Steven was concerned, that was the only service they offered. He would always walk out of there with a shot to the ass or arm. Steven's mother would be asked to pay a nominal fee, and Steven would exit the place, crying.

The *Clínica Médica Familiar* was booming with business until the Superior Medical Clinic opened its doors across the street. The Superior Medical Clinic catered to the same clientele, only the doctor there didn't charge much of a nominal fee, just slightly less than the competition across the street. She was creative. Because of the fact that she worked at another office in a city that was inhabited by insured patients, she was able to overcharge the insurance of those patients in order to compensate for the lack of payment from the patients that frequented the Superior Medical Clinic. While some patients insisted on giving the doctor something for her work, it was usually just enough to cover the cost of keeping the place open and staffed, and a little something for the doctor's time. And, just enough to cover lunch. There was a Tacos Mexico nearby, after all. Steven hated that place, as well. Steven's mother took him there to get his leg fixed. She would also take him there to get shots.

Steven wasn't the only person that got shots at Superior Medical Clinic. The doctor, Doctor Lorenzo, also got shots there. She got two of them, not to the ass or arm, but to the head, and not by a syringe, but by a gun.

The gun belonged to an x-ray technician named Ray. Ray was new to the medical group to which Doctor Lorenzo belonged, in the more lucrative office. He had recently been evaluated by the doctor. She gave him a negative evaluation due to his poor customer relation skills and his inability to arrive to work on time. Both of Ray's negative qualities were due to his alcoholism. Doctor Lorenzo was not aware of Ray's alcoholism. She became aware of it on the day of her death. She received a phone call from her receptionist while out at lunch. The receptionist said, "Doctor Lorenzo? Ray is here and he wants to speak with you about his evaluation. He says he works with you at the other office."

"Ray? Well, I'm about to have lunch." She had just ordered some tacos at Tacos Mexico.

"He's here, now, and he insists that he speak with you. He's really upset," then whispered, "And I think he's drunk."

"He's drunk?"

"I think so. He smells drunk."

Doctor Lorenzo could hear Ray speaking in the background. "I'm not fucking drunk! I want to talk to the doctor. I want to talk with her! Tell her that I want to talk with her! Tell her that I'm not drunk!"

"Doctor Lorenzo? He says that he isn't drunk and that he wants to talk with you."

"Tell him I'll be right there." Dr. Lorenzo got the attention of a singing cook and asked him to pack her tacos to go.

The receptionist did as she was told, as did the cook. Ray continued babbling on about the doctor and what may be the result of her negative evaluation. "I have a family to feed. It's not my fault. Maybe I drink a little, but it's not my fault. I have a family to feed. I have to work. We'll be evicted."

"Ray. The doctor will be here soon. Just relax."

"Don't tell me to fucking relax! I have a family to feed. I can't relax. I have to talk to the doctor. I have to talk to the fucking doctor!"

This went on until the doctor arrived. Ray saw Doctor Lorenzo arrive. Doctor Lorenzo saw Ray when she arrived, only she immediately went into her office. She saw that his eyes were watery. She figured it had something to do with his inebriation, not his sorrow. She had a granola bar in her desk that she wanted to get to before she spoke with Ray. She was on her lunch, after all. She didn't want to eat her tacos just yet because her tacos had onions on them, and she didn't want to have offensive breath when talking with Ray.

When Ray saw Doctor Lorenzo walk into her office, he pulled out a revolver. The receptionist saw him do so, and immediately ran from behind the counter. The receptionist wasn't sure about what she was about to do, but she ran out from behind the counter, anyway. Several patients waiting for the doctor also saw Ray pull out the gun. Some of the smart ones got up and ran for the door. Others screamed. Still, others remained seated, petrified.

The receptionist ran up to Ray and grabbed his revolver-totting arm. She still wasn't sure what she was going to do. Doctor Lorenzo, as she was about to reach for her granola bar, heard the commotion. She turned to the door and opened it. The swing of the door hit the shoulder of the wrestling receptionist at such an angle that it weakened her grip of Ray just enough to allow him to free his arm, point the gun at the doctor, and fire three shots at the doctor's head. One shot missed, two sank and settled in the mass of her brain.

Seeing this, the remaining patients fled the building. The receptionist screamed and, again, grasped at Ray. She still wasn't sure what she was doing. This time, however, Ray saw her coming and shot her in the throat. The receptionist fell to the floor. At that moment, as she attempted to inhale her last breath, she knew what she was doing.

All of the commotion drew the attention of a medical assistant that was in another office eating some tacos that she bought at Tacos Mexico. She came out to take a look at what was causing all the noise only to see Ray turn in her direction. She then heard a bang and saw a puff of smoke and what she thought was a gnat flying toward her face. That was the last sound, sight, and thought she would ever have.

Ray didn't know what to do. He figured he should leave. There were three dead people inside the clinic and a bunch of living people running outside of the clinic. He wanted to be among the living. He went outside.

Upon exiting, he heard people yelling, "There he is," "Call the police," "Get him! This fucking retard is drunk and crazy!" Ray didn't like the sound of that. He wanted to leave. He wanted to get into his car and drive away. He wanted to drive as far as his car would get him. He wanted to forget about his wife and his children and his dog and his apartment across the street from Art's Liquor.

He fumbled for his keys, but the screaming people around him made his hands shake. There was no way he was going to be able to get to his keys out of his pocket with his hands shaking so much, much less maneuver the key into the tiny sliver that the door lock allows. So he did the only thing that he was capable of doing to get him out of this mess. He didn't think about it. He didn't steady himself. He raised the gun to his temple and pulled the trigger.

It was all over the news. When Steven's mother saw a report about it, she cried and cried, and wished she had on some clothes to help her wipe away the tears. All she could do was look over at naked Bob and say, "God bless her," then look back at the television and say, "God bless you, Doctor Lorenzo." All Bob could do was finish his beer.

She told Steven about the incident, but Steven couldn't remember who Dr. Lorenzo was. Steven's mother said, "You know, the doctor. The one that gave you shots and helped fix your leg? God rest her precious soul."

"Muh leg... Muh-muh, my leh-leg. Muh knee... Muh-muh, muh leg."

"Yes, God rest her soul, that one. She's dead."

"Muh leg... Muh-muh, my leh-leg. Muh knee... Muh-muh, muh leg."."

"Yes. She was killed. She's with my Heavenly Father now. Do you remember her? We used to go get Chinese food after seeing her? At the Chinatown Express? Remember the orange chicken?"

That much Steven remembered. He also remembered the Chinatown Express as he made his way past both clinics, on his way toward the train tracks. In fact, he almost decided to stop at the Chinatown Express on his way to the train tracks. He remembered that he was hungry, but just as quickly he remembered the last time he ate at Chinatown Express. Specifically, the orange chicken.

It was his favorite Chinese dish, until he ate it at Chinatown Express. There, the orange chicken was drenched in pink sauce, not orange. Not only was the sauce pink, the meat beneath the sauce and the moist batter that covered it was also pink. That was when Chinatown Express really lived-up to its name. Sure, the food service was quick: they kept everything in steam trays and micro-waved each combination plate before giving it to their customers. They were quick, express-like, if you will. The only thing faster than the service was the speed in which the pink, orange chicken exited Steven's ass. That was quick, express-like, if you will. Steven was sick for days. The pink, orange chicken was shat within minutes: there was orange and pink and brown and black and gray. What remained came later in the form of yellow and brown foam. Steven would never eat there again.

Similar to the first and last time Steven ate a hot dog from a street vendor in Mexico. He imagined they would be delicious based on the smell alone: the bacon crisping in its own grease, hugging a plumping wiener, threatening to burst at the pursed tips. Once topped until unrecognizable, the taste was unlike anything else. It was the aftermath that kept him from ever eating a Mexican hot dog, again. Even after the first flush, enough residual shards of crap remained so that the toilet looked like somebody had cracked a piñata over the commode. It was a mess unlike anything else. The only thing worse was the result of eating a two item combo where both items were orange chicken, his usual order at Chinatown Express, which he had on his last visit.

With hunger, he almost decided to get a two item combo where both items were orange chicken, but he remembered the pink, orange chicken and the Chinatown Express that he became. But it was the bottles that really made him reconsider. He had to get to those labels soon. He had to get to the tracks soon. His hunger would have to wait. His mother would have to wait. However, if all went well, she wouldn't have to wait much longer.

Chapter XVIII

Steven limped, as fast as he could limp, to the train tracks. They were only a few blocks away, off of Ferguson. The box of empty Heineken bottles clinked with every step and drag.

In order for him to have access to the train tracks, he had to walk through an apartment complex. The apartments were on Ferguson, which ran parallel with the tracks. Every property on the south side of that street had its back to the tracks. That made all the apartments and homes on that street cheap to rent and own. A train came by every few minutes. The trains that came by rarely carried passengers. The trains that came by were freight trains, so the steady churning and pounding of the train and seemingly incessant blaring of its horn would last longer than one who wasn't used to it could handle. Steven could handle it. He only lived two blocks away. The people on Ferguson learned to live with the sound for the sake of sleep and for the sake of their wallets.

The apartment complex that Steven had to walk through housed tenants that knew Steven. That is to say, they knew of Steven. Steven walked in and through the apartment complex often, but he never walked back to exit through them. He went toward the end of block, through a different apartment complex, when he needed to make his way back home.

This apartment complex was opposite the side of the tracks from where his bottle collection was. The tenants didn't seem to mind that Steven cut through. If they did, they never told Steven anything. They would see him walk through their driveway, straight through to the back of the apartment building, which had a chain link fence that had been cut, in order for people to have access to the train tracks. Some kids who wanted access to the train tracks so they could ride their bikes along the dirt paths that ran along the tracks cut the fence years ago. The kids also wanted a place to smoke marijuana, drink beer, and screw without fear of a police officer creeping up on them. Unfortunately, for the tenants of the apartments, the opening in the fence also lent itself to vagrants who just happened by the tracks and people who just come off the street seeking a short cut. Steven was one of those people. The tenants never complained to the landlord. It didn't affect the tenants. The rent was cheap. They didn't have anything of value that could be stolen. It wasn't an issue. The landlord, although aware of the opening, never mended the fence because the tenants never complained. Apparently, it wasn't an issue.

It certainly wasn't an issue when Steven walked through, not even when he walked through carrying a twelve pack of sweaty Heineken bottles. He always walked through the apartments carrying some bottles. All the tenants ever said was, "There goes that retarded drunk. Damn, he drinks a lot." They obviously didn't know that Steven was always carrying empty bottles for his bottle collection. Steven didn't know that the tenants didn't know about his bottle collection. He always strolled across the apartments hoping that the tenants didn't see the stash he was carrying. He often wondered, after having walked through, if they did, in fact, see him carrying his bottles and if they themselves wondered where he was stashing all those empty bottles. They didn't.

After Steven made it across the apartments and went through the hole in the fence, he let out a sigh of relief. It's rare that he has a twelve pack of freshly drunk bottles of anything, much less Heineken, with its beautiful, green bottles—even though there were only ten. As far as Steven was concerned, he was in the clear once he made it across the tracks. Once across, he would be only a few yards away from his collection.

There was a train coming. It was still about a mile away. Steven heard it blaring its horn at a distant intersection. Normally, Steven would wait for the train to pass, regardless of how far away it was. He never wanted to risk it. This time, however, because time was of the essence, what with ten fresh bottles sweating away in their Heineken box, he crossed the train tracks.

Steven saw the paper factory wall come up from behind the dune on which the train tracks ran. He was excited. The sun was reaching that pivotal point. He had nearly an hour to peel his labels. It would be hard to do it in that amount of time, but Steven felt he could do it. He really wanted to do it. He wanted to see the sun shine through his collection of bottles, a collection more complete than he has ever had. He would eventually add rows as he collected more bottles, but, until then, his current collection would easily suffice.

It would have sufficed, rather, because as Steven got closer to his collection, he realized that it was gone.

Gone.

Gone.

It was gone. He dropped his Kmart bag.

At first, Steven looked around, perhaps, as improbable as it may be, thinking they might have moved themselves, or perhaps he was looking in the wrong place, across the wrong tracks, against the wall of the wrong paper factory. But he wasn't. He realized this when he saw that there were still a few empty, label-free bottles laying around the floor—some broken—a couple of brown forty-ounce bottles still up against the wall. The rest had vanished.

Steven heard the familiar clink of glass on glass. It was a bottle. Even he, a retard, surmised that in order for glass to clink that way, there had to be more than one. He turned toward the sound and saw an old man in a long, white robe, with long hair and a long beard, bending over to place a few bottles on the rack beneath a Super-A shopping cart that was otherwise filed with bottles, label-less bottles, Steven's bottles. His yearning for their beauty had never been more apparent when he saw how the sun shone through their round, imperfect translucence. The old man was mumbling something as he quickly placed some of the bottles back on top of the rest of the bottles in the cart, and yanked at the cart, allowing several bottles to fall with a crash onto the ground. Steven had to react, but he couldn't move. The train was only a few yards away. It was blaring its horn intensely.

Steven didn't know what to do. He thought for a second, but nothing came to his mind. He recognized the old man in the long, white robe, with long hair and a long beard. He recognized him as the man with which his mother was in cahoots. The one to which she would whisper, mostly on bended knee, occasionally with her eyes closed. The second mastermind behind the plan that Mickey had mentioned, to rid Steven of his bottles. His mother sent the old man. He must have been hauling the bottles all day long, and this was his last batch.

He had been hauling the bottles all day. That much was true. He wasn't, however, in cahoots with Steven's mother. He wasn't Jesus Christ. He was Jim, a local transient that has been a part of the neighborhood longer than Steven. In fact, his name wasn't even Jim. People around the neighborhood just called him Jim because they didn't know what else to call him. Had they ever bothered to ask him, he would have told them that his name was J. J. Christianson, Nick the drunk's brother. Had they inquired into his initials, he would have told them that the first J was for Jonathan, the second J was for Jesus, no less. Steven had seen him before, but he was usually draped in a loose, stained, gray sweater, or blanket. Jim had recently discovered the long white robe while fumbling in the dumpster behind the Superior Medical Clinic. He was just recycling bottles the way he has been for years. He just sort of hit the jackpot upon stumbling on Steven's collection.

Steven yelled at the man, "He-here! He-He-Here! Buh-back! Buh-bu-back! He-here! Cuh-cuh-come! Cuh-cuh-come! He-he-here!" Steven considered running after him, but the train was nearly above him, its horn a painful scream in Steven's head.

Steven stared through the train, watching the man pushing the cart through the spaces between the carriages, gradually shrinking off in the distance between flickers like in some poorly produced student film. Steven couldn't do anything. He had a headache. He was hungry. He hated his mother. He wanted to cry. She was going to pay for this. She was going to pay for this. She was going to pay for this. He had to wait for the train to pass. There wasn't anything Steven could do, so he did what he always did when he didn't have anything to do and he felt as though he wanted to cry: he cried.

Chapter XIX

Steven continued to cry long after the train had passed. He thought about his bottles. He thought about his mother. He thought about Mickey. He looked at his watch. He thought about his mother. He thought about Jesus. He thought about his bottles.

Steven looked at the empty wall of the paper factory. At that moment, the sun was shining on it. Had his bottle collection still been there, it would have been illuminated with brilliant ambers, greens, and whites. It would have been perfect. As close to complete as he's ever had it. But it wasn't. It was just sunlight on a white wall, and nothing else. It was all his mother's doing. It was all his mother's fault.

Steven decided it was time to do what Mickey had told him to do. Only now, it wasn't to protect his collection, it was to make sure that it never happened again, and to make sure that his mother pays for what she has done. It was time for Steven to go home. There was no reason for him to stay at the tracks. No reason.

He got up, pulled up at his dirty T-shirt collar to wipe his eyes, and walked over to the wall of the paper factory and aligned the few remaining bottles against the wall. If he was going to start over, he had to start now. He picked up the stray ones that were scattered around and saw, for a few seconds, the sunlight shine through them. It was nice, and well worth the minimal effort that it took to do that, but it wasn't perfect.

Steven ignored the twelve pack of Heineken that was

quickly drying on the floor. He would get to it later. Steven picked up his Kmart bag, and he walked back across the tracks and through the different apartment complex—the ones he always walked through after visiting his bottles. He walked east on Ferguson, toward Garfield, because he wanted a Snickers bar. It was time for one. He was hungry. That Snickers bar would satisfy him, or so he heard that on television. He walked toward Art's Liquor because that was where he always bought his Snickers bars.

As he made his way toward Art's Liquor, he discarded the Kmart bag that held his new knife. He wanted to get a feel for the handle. He wanted to make sure that it felt natural in his hand, though since he never before held a knife in his hand, he wasn't sure what the natural feel was. He really just wanted to be sure that he had a good grip so that it didn't slip. He wanted to make sure that as he stabbed into his mother's chest, that his hand didn't slip off the handle, causing his hand to grip the blade. That would hurt a lot, and he didn't want any more pain.

He walked into Art's Liquor with the knife in hand. He saw that Tony Chafas was sitting behind the counter. Tony was eating a piece of beef jerky. Steven was crying.

Tony saw Steven as he walked in with a knife, crying, which made Tony shift a bit in his seat.

"Hey, Steven. What's up?"

Steven mumbled something to Tony in his usual retarded way. Tony translated Steven's mumbles as best he could—which is to say, not very well at all—only Steven was crying, which made things even more impossible to understand, if that's even possible. Steven walked past Tony and grabbed a Snickers bar off of the tiered shelves. He then took the Snickers bar to the counter.

Steven was waving around the knife and his Snickers Bar saying, "Fuh-fuh-fuck... Muh-muh-motherfuh-fuh-fuck. Fuh-fuh-fucker... Muh-mother... Muh-muh-motherfuck. I'll, I'll, I'll kuh-kuh-kill, kill'em. Kuh-kuh-kuh-kill'em. I'll kill'em. Muh-muh-motherfuh-fuh-fuck."

Tony didn't know what to make of what Steven was saying, this time, and made little effort to try what with Steven's retardation, and all. Tony wondered if Steven was telling Tony that he'd kill him: Tony. Had Tony tried to ask Steven to explain what was wrong, Tony wouldn't have understood him anyway. He still would have pretended to understand. All Tony thought to say was, "Seventy-five cents," the price of the Snickers Bar.

Steven gave Tony a wrinkled dollar, while adding, "I'll, I'll, I'll kuh-kuh-kill, kill'em."

Tony gave Steven a quarter in change, which was the extent to which Tony wanted any involvement into whatever was going on in this retard's mind at the time. Steven took the quarter, thought to tell Tony his plan of action once more, but he thought better of it. Instead, he walked away, mumbling and crying as he went out the door.

Had Steven walked through the parking lot behind Art's Liquor, he would have seen that Jim, the transient, had all of Steven's bottles back there, in bags and boxes against Art's Liquor's trash bin. But Steven didn't walk through the parking lot of Art's Liquor. He continued walking on the sidewalk, north on Garfield, and made a left onto Southside, toward his mother's house.

As Steven walked and limped, he noticed, on several occasions, that there were bottles along the gutter, on the grass, in brown bags against the trees. He even saw several of his neighbors sitting on their porches drinking beer and soda out of bottles. They seemed, to Steven, to magnify in the hands of his neighbors, their guzzles and refreshing sighs amplified. His eyes became telescopes as he saw the wet bottles in their hands, then microscopes, as he saw that some of the labels on the bottles were lifting on the corners. He wanted to stop and ask his neighbors if he could have the bottles once they were through with them, that he would wait as they drank them, and then gladly take the bottles from them, to save them the trip to the garbage can. Then Steven would find a quiet place to peel the labels off and save them for his collection. But it didn't seem important, at the time. He had other things to do. He ate his Snickers as he walked past all of these neighbors, and all of their bottles. He even ignored the recycling bins that the city provided in order to ensure that its residents recycled. Had the bins been out yesterday, Steven would have rummaged through them, with hopes that out of the dozens of bins, he might find one solitary bottle with a forgiving label that he could add to his collection. But he didn't rummage through the bins. He had other things to do. Had he bothered to look through the bins, he wouldn't have found any bottles anyway because Jim, the transient, had already gotten to them.

Steven had no way of knowing what was in the recycling bins. And, at the moment, he didn't really care.

Even the recycling bin in front of his house was out on the curb, awaiting disposal by the city's sanitation department. There had to be dozens of empty bottles in that can, what with

Bob and Steven's mother being alcoholics. He didn't check it. He walked right into the back yard, toward his garage. He had to tell Mickey what had happened. He had to tell Mickey that he was right. He had to tell Mickey that it was time to kill his mother. It was time.

On his way to his garage, Steven heard the familiar song coming from inside the house:

> Bad boys, bad boys,
> Whatcha gonna do,
> Whatcha gonna do
> When they come for you?
> Bad boys, bad boys,
> Whatcha gonna do,
> Whatcha gonna do
> When they come for you?

Hearing the song, Steven knew that Bob was home. Then again, Bob was always home. Since it was getting dark, his mother should be home. If she wasn't, she would be getting home very soon. She would wonder why Steven hadn't eaten his chorizo burrito. She wouldn't go out and ask him why he hadn't eaten it. She would just wonder.

When Steven entered his bedroom in the garage, he noticed that something was different. He felt it. Something was different. Mickey was still lying on the bed, the sheets pulled up just above his waist, but he was tilted over. Mickey's eyes appeared to be looking just above the bed. Steven's collection of boogers had been wiped away, mostly. There was still a bit of residue from those that had petrified to the extent that they would have to be soaked and softened with a warm rag for a few minutes before they could be wiped or chipped away. He looked on the floor and saw that some of the dust bunnies, especially those that had collected near his door, had disappeared. Steven's eyes went from the floor to his chest of drawers. That was when Steven saw that his top drawer had been left open. This would not be good.

Chapter XX

Steven looked in his top drawer and saw that all of the women's underwear that he had accumulated had vanished, and he never even had a chance to give them to his mother. He looked in the drawers below, just in case, even though he knew that the underwear could not have climbed out of the top drawer and made its way to any of the other drawers. He checked, anyway. He was retarded. For a second he imagined that all of the women who owned the underwear that he had taken came and found their underwear, that they waited in a long line, occasionally looked at their watches because they had better things to do, but waited nonetheless, and claimed panties. But, his pills were also missing. This meant that his mother had come into his room because those pills belonged solely to Steven. Nobody would get in line for those. It meant that his mother knew that he hadn't taken them. It meant that his mother would soon confront him, that she would be disappointed in him, that she would possibly yell at him, and pray to God, no doubt. She would ask way too many questions that Steven would never be able to answer. Still, there was a chance that it may have been somebody else. He needed answers. Steven was very uncomfortable.

Steven looked at Mickey and asked him, "Wh-wh-what . . . What? Wh-who? Wha-wha-wha-what?" Steven was trying to ask Mickey who it was that had entered his room.

Mickey remained still, staring directly ahead, his permanent smile making his silence conspicuous.

Steven knew that Mickey knew who was in the room. Steven just had to guess.

"Wha-wha-wha . . . Wha . . . Mo-mo-mom?" Steven was asking if it was his mother who was in his room.

Mickey remained silent, staring directly ahead, smiling. Steven knew what this meant. This meant that it was his mother that was in the room.

"Duh-duh-do you . . . Do-do yuh-you . . . Boh-boh-boh-bottles . . . Boh-boh-boh-bottles?" Steven asked if Mickey knew that his bottle collection was missing.

Mickey remained silent, staring directly ahead, smiling. Steven knew what this meant. This meant that Mickey knew that Steven's bottles were missing because Mickey had anticipated it. He knew that the bottles would soon vanish. That was why he told Steven that he had to kill his mother.

"Whu-whu-what . . . Whatah . . . Whu-whu-whatah . . . Bob?" Steven was asking if Bob had anything to do with it, with the missing bottles, and his newly tidy room. Not that Bob was any kind of mastermind or anything. Bob just never had much to do, so he had to be a part of anything that was going on at home.

Mickey remained silent, staring directly ahead, smiling. Steven knew what this meant. This meant that Bob was completely in on the whole thing. Bob was just as guilty as Steven's mother. Bob had to be dealt with, as well.

"Kuh-kuh-kuh-kill'em . . . Kuh-kuh-kill'em?"

Mickey remained silent, staring directly ahead, smiling.

Steven left his room. He was crying, but not for the bottles. He was crying because he was mad. He was madder than he had ever been. He was madder than that time he threw his dog against the wall. He was mad at his mother and Bob and Jesus because they stole his bottles. He was mad at his mother for taking the underwear that he was collecting in order to give to her. He was mad because his mother was going to be mad at him after finding out that he hasn't taken a single little, blue pill. He was mad at the fact that he had to take pills. He was mad because Mickey knew everything, and Steven, the retard that he is, knew absolutely nothing. He was mad because he was retarded.

Steven had his knife. He decided to walk through the back door, which led into his mother's bedroom. This way, he could walk through the bedroom, into the living room, and surprise them. No planning in the world could prepare them for this. They wouldn't see it coming. Steven did just that.

In the living room, Bob was sitting on his naked ass, drinking a beer, and watching another episode of Cops. Bob had his legs crossed, so his schlong had dropped within the shadows of his legs and his bushy pubes. Steven heard the theme song. There must have been a Cops marathon on television. He saw that Bob was holding a bottle. The bottle's label was facing Bob, so Steven swore that Bob must have been holding a label-free bottle, a bottle from his collection. Bob was humming along while taking a swig of beer:

> Bad boys, bad boys,
> Whatcha gonna do,
> Whatcha gonna do
> When they come for you?
> Bad boys, bad boys,
> Whatcha gonna do,

> Whatcha gonna do
> When they come for you?

Steven didn't think twice. He knew what he had to do. Bob didn't know anything. Steven's mother wasn't in the room. This was good for Steven because he had to kill one at a time. Bob could be first. It didn't really matter.

Bob barely saw it coming. He didn't have time to stare at Steven. Steven just walked directly in front of Bob, held-up the knife, and stabbed Bob twice in the face, one stab in each eye. Steven thought Bob didn't see it coming, but he did. He didn't know what it was, or why it was, but he saw it coming. Each time the blade came toward each of his eyes, although very quickly, he saw the blade until a millisecond before it penetrated his eyeball. Lucky for Steven, and Bob, the blade was long enough to pierce through the eyes, and into the brain, which was possible because the knife was just narrow enough. Lucky he didn't buy a wide hunting knife like Rambo's. Lucky.

Bob barely had a second to let out a girlish yelp before he died. Steven didn't yell. He grunted several times, and then took a step back, blood splattered across his face, and said, "Muh-muh-motherfuck. I'll, I'll, I'll kuh-kuh-kill, kill." Bob would never get the opportunity to stare at Steven with functioning eyes, again. He just sat on the couch, his head slightly tilted, his eyes dripping blood. Bob's face was turned in Steven's direction, but Bob wasn't looking.

Steven's mother made the mistake of reacting to the noises she heard. It was a mistake because her reaction caused her to step into the living room, nervously tying on her robe.

There, she saw Steven. Bloody knife and face, and Bob, just bloody face.

She screamed. "Oh, God! Oh, God! Jesus! Oh, God!" She then backed into the dining room. Steven patiently followed her.

When Steven walked into the dining room, he saw a pile of women's underwear on the table, and a pile of his little, blue pills in a salad bowl. He saw that his mother was holding the porcelain figure of Jesus Christ that she always prayed to, in one hand, while she placed the telephone down with the other.

"Why, Steven? Good Lord, Jesus, Heavenly Father, why?" She was sobbing. Her face was cringed and her back was hunched. "Why, Steven? What's wrong, Steven? Why did you kill my husband? Why? Good Lord, Jesus, why? What's wrong?"

Steven thought he might say something, but didn't. He just looked at the floor, then back at her.

"Why, Steven? Why haven't you been taking your pills? Why? If you would have taken your pills, this would have never happened. Why didn't you take your pills? Now look at what you have done. God, why did this happen?"

Steven didn't know where to look. He actually started feeling bad. He wasn't sure why he felt bad. He knew he didn't like to see his mother cry. Seeing her cry had made him sort of forget that she had taken his bottles. He was feeling sorry for having stabbed Bob.

Steven pointed at the pile of women's underwear on the table. "Yuh-yuh-you . . . Yuh-you, yuh-yuh-yuh-you, you. Foh-foh-for you."

"Underwear? Whose are these? Mrs. Montes'? Whose?"

"Yuh-yuh-yuh . . . You." Steven continued pointing at the underwear.

"These aren't mine, Steven. Don't you understand? God, Jesus, Lord and Savior, please."

Steven's mother looked beyond Steven. There was a wall behind him, but she was looking in the general direction of where her dead husband sat, naked. She held up the statue of Jesus Christ. She regained her composure, slightly. "Ask for forgiveness, Steven. Ask Him for forgiveness. He'll forgive you, Steven. Ask Him, please, Steven. Ask Him! Ask Him! Ask Him!" The third time she said it, she said it with such fervor, that the statue fell to the floor with a crash.

The sound of the statue hitting the floor reminded Steven as to why he was there. He looked at his Mickey Mouse watch. Mickey was looking at him. It was 9 pm. Mickey's short arm was pointing in the direction of Steven's left hand, which held the bloody knife. Mickey's long arm was pointing at Steven's mother. Steven knew what he had to do. He did it. One stab through her heart. She cringed and hunched over as though she had a pain in her stomach. She fell to the ground.

"Why, Steven? Lord, Jesus, why? Why didn't you take your pills? Take your pills, Steven. Take your pills. Take your pills. Take your pills. Take your pills. Take . . ."

Steven had done what it was he had set out to do. Steven didn't know what else he had to do, so he took his little, blue pills—all of them. He grabbed handfuls of his little, blue pills and stuffed them in his mouth like movie theater popcorn, only much more bitter, chalky, coarse. He chewed and swallowed and chewed and swallowed some more, until they were all gone. Within minutes, he fell to the floor.

He fell so that his head lay right next to his dead mother's, his arms at his waist. It was 9:15 pm. Mickey's short arm was pointing at Steven. His long arm was pointing at Steven's mother. Steven didn't see this. He was staring straight up to the ceiling, but not really looking at anything but blurry light. He was vomiting. He wasn't vomiting violently. Vomit was just pouring out of a corner of his mouth, along the side of his face. His head was surrounded by a bluish, green pool with a few peanuts, chocolate, and caramel.

The last things he would hear were sirens, and then pounding at his mother's front door. The last things he would see were the dark, fuzzy shape of a police officer clapping his hands above Steven's face, that image crisscrossing traces of the figure, then silhouettes. He couldn't hear the clapping. He felt a buzzing in his cheeks and gums that grew more ferocious with every second, until the vibrations became an incessant buzzing in his ears that threatened a never-ending crescendo. Steven thought he might try telling the police officer something—to explain what he had done, and why he had to do it, and that he had no choice. But he didn't. He knew that he couldn't, even if he wanted to. There was no point. The police officer wouldn't understand him, anyway.

CPSIA information can be obtained
at www.ICGtesting.com
Printed in the USA
LVHW04s1718101018
593122LV00001B/224/P